ON THE TRAIL OF EVIL MEN:

So close were the two canoes that Kaviri had only an opportunity to note the white face of Tarzan in the bow of the oncoming craft before his men were on their feet, yelling like mad devils and thrusting their long spears at the occupants of the other canoe.

But a moment later Kaviri would have given all that he possessed to have been safely within his distant village. From the bottom of the ape-man's canoe rose the frightful apes of Akut, growling and barking, with long, hairy arms outstretched to grasp the menacing spears. As the canoes touched, Tarzan spoke to Sheeta and Akut.

With a blood-freezing scream, a huge panther sprang upon them, wreaking fearful havoc with his mighty talons and long, sharp fangs, while Akut buried his yellow canines in the neck of those that came within his reach . . .

Edgar Rice Burroughs
TARZAN NOVELS

TARZAN OF THE APES (#1)
THE RETURN OF TARZAN (#2)
THE BEASTS OF TARZAN (#3)
THE SON OF TARZAN (#4)
TARZAN AND THE JEWELS OF OPAR (#5)
JUNGLE TALES OF TARZAN #6)
TARZAN THE UNTAMED (#7)
TARZAN THE TERRIBLE (#8)
TARZAN AND THE GOLDEN LION (#9)
TARZAN AND THE ANT MEN (#10)
TARZAN, LORD OF THE JUNGLE (#11)
TARZAN AND THE LOST EMPIRE (#12)
TARZAN AT THE EARTH'S CORE (#13)
TARZAN THE INVINCIBLE (#14)
TARZAN TRIUMPHANT (#15)
TARZAN AND THE CITY OF GOLD (#16)
TARZAN AND THE LION MAN (#17)
TARZAN AND THE LEOPARD MEN (#18)
TARZAN'S QUEST (#19)
TARZAN AND THE FORBIDDEN CITY (#20)
TARZAN THE MAGNIFICENT (#21)
TARZAN AND THE FOREIGN LEGION (#22)
TARZAN AND THE MADMAN (#23)
TARZAN AND THE CASTAWAYS (#24)

COMPLETE AND UNABRIDGED!

THE BEASTS OF TARZAN

Edgar Rice Burroughs

BALLANTINE BOOKS • NEW YORK

To
JOAN BURROUGHS

CONTENTS

CHAPTER		PAGE
I	Kidnapped	7
II	Marooned	13
III	Beasts at Bay	21
IV	Sheeta	30
V	Mugambi	38
VI	A Hideous Crew	45
VII	Betrayed	53
VIII	The Dance of Death	60
IX	Chivalry or Villainy	67
X	The Swede	75
XI	Tambudza	82
XII	A Black Scoundrel	89
XIII	Escape	96
XIV	Alone in the Jungle	102
XV	Down the Ugambi	109
XVI	In the Darkness of the Night	116
XVII	On the Deck of the "Kincaid"	123
XVIII	Paulvitch Plots Revenge	129
XIX	The Last of the "Kincaid"	138
XX	Jungle Island Again	142
XXI	The Law of the Jungle	150

1

Kidnapped

"THE entire affair is shrouded in mystery," said D'Arnot. "I have it on the best of authority that neither the police nor the special agents of the general staff have the faintest conception of how it was accomplished. All they know, all that anyone knows, is that Nikolas Rokoff has escaped."

John Clayton, Lord Greystoke—he who had been "Tarzan of the Apes"—sat in silence in the apartments of his friend, Lieutenant Paul D'Arnot, in Paris, gazing meditatively at the toe of his immaculate boot.

His mind revolved many memories, recalled by the escape of his arch-enemy from the French military prison to which he had been sentenced for life upon the testimony of the ape-man.

He thought of the lengths to which Rokoff had once gone to compass his death, and he realized that what the man had already done would doubtless be as nothing by comparison with what he would wish and plot to do now that he was again free.

Tarzan had recently brought his wife and infant son to London to escape the discomforts and dangers of the rainy season upon their vast estate in Uziri—the land of the savage Waziri warriors whose broad African domains the ape-man had once ruled.

He had run across the Channel for a brief visit with his old friend, but the news of the Russian's escape had already cast a shadow upon his outing, so that though he had but just arrived he was already contemplating an immediate return to London.

"It is not that I fear for myself, Paul," he said at last.

"Many times in the past have I thwarted Rokoff's designs upon my life; but now there are others to consider. Unless I misjudge the man, he would more quickly strike at me through my wife or son than directly at me, for he doubtless realizes that in no other way could he inflict greater anguish upon me. I must go back to them at once, and remain with them until Rokoff is recaptured—or dead."

As these two talked in Paris, two other men were talking together in a little cottage upon the outskirts of London. Both were dark, sinister-looking men.

One was bearded, but the other, whose face wore the pallor of long confinement within doors, had but a few days' growth of black beard upon his face. It was he who was speaking.

"You must needs shave off that beard of yours, Alexis," he said to his companion. "With it he would recognize you on the instant. We must separate here in the hour, and when we meet again upon the deck of the *Kincaid*, let us hope that we shall have with us two honoured guests who little anticipate the pleasant voyage we have planned for them.

"In two hours I should be upon my way to Dover with one of them, and by tomorrow night, if you follow my instructions carefully, you should arrive with the other, provided, of course, that he returns to London as quickly as I presume he will.

"There should be both profit and pleasure as well as other good things to reward our efforts, my dear Alexis. Thanks to the stupidity of the French, they have gone to such lengths to conceal the fact of my escape for these many days that I have had ample opportunity to work out every detail of our little adventure so carefully that there is little chance of the slightest hitch occuring to mar our prospects. And now good-bye, and good luck!"

Three hours later a messenger mounted the steps to the apartment of Lieutenant Paul D'Arnot.

"A telegram for Lord Greystoke," he said to the servant who answered his summons. "Is he here?"

The man answered in the affirmative, and, signing for the message, carried it within to Tarzan, who was already preparing to depart for London.

Tarzan tore open the envelope, and as he read his face went white.

"Read it, Paul," he said, handing the slip of paper to D'Arnot. "It has come already."

The Frenchman took the telegram and read:

"Jack stolen from garden through complicity of new servant. Come at once.—JANE."

As Tarzan leaped from the roadster that had met him at the station and ran up the steps to his London town house he was met at the door by a dry-eyed but almost frantic woman.

Quickly Jane Porter Clayton narrated all that she had been able to learn of the theft of the boy.

The baby's nurse had been wheeling him in the sunshine on the walk before the house when a closed taxicab drew up at the corner of the street. The woman had paid but passing attention to the vehicle, merely noting that it discharged no passenger, but stood at the kerb with the motor running as though waiting for a fare from the residence before which it had stopped.

Almost immediately the new houseman, Carl, had come running from the Greystoke house, saying that the girl's mistress wished to speak with her for a moment, and that she was to leave little Jack in his care until she returned.

The woman said that she entertained not the slightest suspicion of the man's motives until she had reached the doorway of the house, when it occurred to her to warn him not to turn the carriage so as to permit the sun to shine in the baby's eyes.

As she turned about to call this to him she was somewhat surprised to see that he was wheeling the carriage rapidly toward the corner, and at the same time she saw the door of the taxicab open and a swarthy face framed for a moment in the aperture.

Intuitively, the danger to the child flashed upon her, and with a shriek she dashed down the steps and up the walk toward the taxicab, into which Carl was now handing the baby to the swarthy one within.

Just before she reached the vehicle, Carl leaped in beside his confederate, slamming the door to behind him. At the same time the chauffeur attempted to start his machine, but it was evident that something had gone wrong, as though the gears refused to mesh, and the delay caused by this, while he pushed the lever into reverse and backed the car a few inches before again attempting to go ahead, gave the nurse time to reach the side of taxicab.

Leaping to the running-board, she had attempted to snatch the baby from the arms of the stranger, and here, screaming and fighting, she had clung to her position even after the taxicab had got under way; nor was it until the machine had passed the Greystoke residence at good speed that Carl, with a heavy blow to her face, had succeeded in knocking her to the pavement.

Her screams had attracted servants and members of the families from residences near by, as well as from the Greystoke home. Lady Greystoke had witnessed the girl's brave battle, and had herself tried to reach the rapidly passing vehicle, but had been too late.

That was all that anyone knew, nor did Lady Greystoke dream of the possible identity of the man at the bottom of the plot until her husband told her of the escape of Nikolas Rokoff from the French prison where they had hoped he was permanently confined.

As Tarzan and his wife stood planning the wisest course to pursue, the telephone bell rang in the library at their right. Tarzan quickly answered the call in person.

"Lord Greystoke?" asked a man's voice at the other end of the line.

"Yes."

"Your son has been stolen," continued the voice, "and I alone may help you to recover him. I am conversant with the plot of those who took him. In fact, I was a party to it, and was to share in the reward, but now they are trying to ditch me, and to be quits with them I will aid you to recover him on condition that you will not prosecute me for my part in the crime. What do you say?"

"If you lead me to where my son is hidden," replied the ape-man, "you need fear nothing from me."

"Good," replied the other. "But you must come alone to meet me, for it is enough that I must trust you. I cannot take the chance of permitting others to learn my identity."

"Where and when may I meet you?" asked Tarzan.

The other gave the name and location of a public-house on the water-front at Dover—a place frequented by sailors.

"Come," he concluded, "about ten o'clock tonight. It would do no good to arrive earlier. Your son will be safe enough in the meantime, and I can then lead you secretly to where he is hidden. But be sure to come alone, and under no circumstances notify Soctland Yard, for I know you well and shall be watching for you.

"Should any other accompany you, or should I see suspicious characters who might be agents of the police, I shall not meet you, and your last chance of recovering your son will be gone."

Without more words the man rang off.

Tarzan repeated the gist of the conversation to his wife. She begged to be allowed to accompany him, but he insisted that it might result in the man's carrying out his threat of refusing to aid them if Tarzan did not come alone, and so they parted, he to hasten to Dover, and she, ostensibly, to wait at home until he should notify her of the outcome of his mission.

Little did either dream of what both were destined to pass through before they should meet again, or the far-distant— but why anticipate?

For ten minutes after the ape-man had left her Jane Clayton walked restlessly back and forth across the silken rugs of the library. Her mother heart ached, bereft of its firstborn. Her mind was in an anguish of hopes and fears.

Though her judgment told her that all would be well were her Tarzan to go alone in accordance with the mysterious stranger's summons, her intuition would not permit her to lay aside suspicion of the gravest dangers to both her husband and her son.

The more she thought of the matter, the more convinced she became that the recent telephone message might be but a ruse to keep them inactive until the boy was safely hidden away or spirited out of England. Or it might be that it had been simply a bait to lure Tarzan into the hands of the implacable Rokoff.

With the lodgment of this thought she stopped in wide-eyed terror. Instantly it became a conviction. She glanced at the great clock ticking the minutes in the corner of the library.

It was too late to catch the Dover train that Tarzan was to take. There was another, later, however, that would bring her to the Channel port in time to reach the address the stranger had given her husband before the appointed hour.

Summoning her maid and chauffeur, she issued instructions rapidly. Ten minutes later she was being whisked through the crowded streets toward the railway station.

It was nine-forty-five that night that Tarzan entered the squalid "pub" on the water-front in Dover. As he passed into the evil-smelling room a muffled figure brushed past him toward the street.

"Come, my lord!" whispered the stranger.

The ape-man wheeled about and followed the other into the ill-lit alley, which custom had dignified with the title of thoroughfare. Once outside, the fellow led the way into the darkness, nearer a wharf, where high-piled bales, boxes, and casks cast dense shadows. Here he halted.

"Where is the boy?" asked Greystoke.

"On that small steamer whose lights you can just see yonder," replied the other.

In the gloom Tarzan was trying to peer into the features of his companion, but he did not recognize the man as one whom he had ever before seen. Had he guessed that his guide was Alexis Paulvitch he would have realized that naught but treachery lay in the man's heart, and that danger lurked in the path of every move.

"He is unguarded now," continued the Russian. "Those who took him feel perfectly safe from detection, and with the exception of a couple of members of the crew, whom I have furnished with enough gin to silence them effectually for hours, there is none aboard the *Kincaid*. We can go aboard, get the child, and return without the slightest fear."

Tarzan nodded.

"Let's be about it, then," he said.

His guide led him to a small boat moored alongside the wharf. The two men entered, and Paulvitch pulled rapidly toward the steamer. The black smoke issuing from her funnel did not at the time make any suggeston to Tarzan's mind. All his thoughts were occupied with the hope that in a few moments he would again have his little son in his arms.

At the steamer's side they found a monkey-ladder dangling close above them, and up this the two men crept stealthily. Once on deck they hastened aft to where the Russian pointed to a hatch.

"The boy is hidden there," he said. "You had better go down after him, as there is less chance that he will cry in fright than should he find himself in the arms of a stranger. I will stand on guard here."

So anxious was Tarzan to rescue the child that he gave not the slightest thought to the strangeness of all the conditions surrounding the *Kincaid*. That her deck was deserted, though she had steam up, and from the volume of smoke pouring from her funnel was all ready to get under way made no impression upon him.

With the thought that in another instant he would fold that precious little bundle of humanity in his arms, the ape-man swung down into the darkness below. Scarcely had he released his hold upon the edge of the hatch than the heavy covering fell clattering above him.

Instantly he knew that he was the victim of a plot, and that far from rescuing his son he had himself fallen into the hands of his enemies. Though he immediately endeavoured to reach the hatch and lift the cover, he was unable to do so.

Striking a match, he explored his surroundings, finding

that a little compartment had been partitioned off from the main hold, with the hatch above his head the only means of ingress or egress. It was evident that the room had been prepared for the very purpose of serving as a cell for himself.

There was nothing in the compartment, and no other occupant. If the child was on board the *Kincaid* he was confined elsewhere.

For over twenty years, from infancy to manhood, the ape-man had roamed his savage jungle haunts without human companionship of any nature. He had learned at the most impressionable period of his life to take his pleasures and his sorrows as the beasts take theirs.

So it was that he neither raved nor stormed against fate, but instead waited patiently for what might next befall him, though not by any means without an eye to doing the utmost to succour himself. To this end he examined his prison carefully, tested the heavy planking that formed its walls, and measured the distance of the hatch above him.

And while he was thus occupied there came suddenly to him the vibration of machinery and the throbbing of the propeller.

The ship was moving! Where to and to what fate was it carrying him?

And even as these thoughts passed through his mind there came to his ears above the din of the engines that which caused him to go cold with apprehension.

Clear and shrill from the deck above him rang the scream of a frightened woman.

2

Marooned

AS Tarzan and his guide had disappeared into the shadows upon the dark wharf the figure of a heavily veiled woman had hurried down the narrow alley to the entrance of the drinking-place the two men had just quitted. Here she paused and looked about, and then as though satisfied that she had at last reached the place she sought, she pushed bravely into the interior of the vile den.

A score of half-drunken sailors and wharf-rats looked up at the unaccustomed sight of a richly gowned woman in their midst. Rapidly she approached the slovenly barmaid who stared half in envy, half in hate, at her more fortunate sister.

"Have you seen a tall, well-dressed man here, but a minute since," she asked, "who met another and went away with him?"

The girl answered in the affirmative, but could not tell which way the two had gone. A sailor who had approached to listen to the conversation vouchsafed the information that a moment before as he had been about to enter the "pub" he had seen two men leaving it who walked toward the wharf.

"Show me the direction they went," cried the woman, slipping a coin into the man's hand.

The fellow led her from the place, and together they walked quickly toward the wharf and along it until across the water they saw a small boat just pulling into the shadows of a near-by steamer.

"There they be," whispered the man.

"Ten pounds if you will find a boat and row me to that steamer," cried the woman.

"Quick, then," he replied, "for we gotta go it if we're goin' to catch the *Kincaid* afore she sails. She's had steam up for three hours an' jest been a-waitin' fer that one passenger. I was a-talkin' to one of her crew 'arf an hour ago."

As he spoke he led the way to the end of the wharf where he knew another boat lay moored, and, lowering the woman into it, he jumped in after and pushed off. The two were soon scudding over the water.

At the steamer's side the man demanded his pay and, without waiting to count out the exact amount, the woman thrust a handful of bank-notes into his outstretched hand. A single glance at them convinced the fellow that he had been more than well paid. Then he assisted her up the ladder, holding his skiff close to the ship's side against the chance that this profitable passenger might wish to be taken ashore later.

But presently the sound of the donkey engine and the rattle of a steel cable on the hoisting-drum proclaimed the fact that the *Kincaid*'s anchor was being raised, and a moment later the waiter heard the propellers revolving, and slowly the little steamer moved away from him out into the channel.

As he turned to row back to shore he heard a woman's shriek from the ship's deck.

"That's wot I calls rotten luck," he soliloquized. "I might jest as well of 'ad the whole bloomin' wad."

When Jane Clayton climbed to the deck of the *Kincaid* she found the ship apparently deserted. There was no sign of those she sought nor of any other aboard, and so she went about her search for her husband and the child she hoped against hope to find there without interruption.

Quickly she hastened to the cabin, which was half above and half below deck. As she hurried down the short companion-ladder into the main cabin, on either side of which were the smaller rooms occupied by the officers, she failed to note the quick closing of one of the doors before her. She passed the full length of the main room, and then retracing her steps stopped before each door to listen, furtively trying each latch.

All was silence, utter silence there, in which the throbbing of her own frightened heart seemed to her overwrought imagination to fill the ship with its thunderous alarm.

One by one the doors opened before her touch, only to reveal empty interiors. In her absorption she did not note the sudden activity upon the vessel, the purring of the engines, the throbbing of the propeller. She had reached the last door upon the right now, and as she pushed it open she was seized from within by a powerful, dark-visaged man, and drawn hastily into the stuffy, ill-smelling interior.

The sudden shock of fright which the unexpected attack had upon her drew a single piercing scream from her throat; then the man clapped a hand roughly over the mouth.

"Not until we are farther from land, my dear," he said. "Then you may yell your pretty head off."

Lady Greystoke turned to look into the leering, bearded face so close to hers. The man relaxed the pressure of his fingers upon her lips, and with a little moan of terror as she recognized him the girl shrank away from her captor.

"Nikolas Rokoff! M. Thuran!" she exclaimed.

"Your devoted admirer," replied the Russian, with a low bow.

"My little boy," she said next, ignoring the terms of endearment—"where is he? Let me have him. How could you be so cruel—even as you—Nikolas Rokoff—cannot be entirely devoid of mercy and compassion? Tell me where he is.

Is he aboard this ship? Oh, please, if such a thing as a heart beats within your breast, take me to my baby!"

"If you do as you are bid no harm will befall him," replied Rokoff. "But remember that it is your own fault that you are here. You came aboard voluntarily, and you may take the consequences. I little thought," he added to himself, "that any such good luck as this would come to me."

He went on deck then, locking the cabin-door upon his prisoner, and for several days she did not see him. The truth of the matter being that Nikolas Rokoff was so poor a sailor that the heavy seas the *Kincaid* encountered from the very beginning of her voyage sent the Russian to his berth with a bad attack of sea-sickness.

During this time her only visitor was an uncouth Swede, the *Kincaid's* unsavoury cook, who brought her meals to her. His name was Sven Anderssen, his one pride being that his patronymic was spelt with a double "s."

The man was tall and raw-boned, with a long yellow moustache, an unwholesome complexion, and filthy nails. The very sight of him with one grimy thumb buried deep in the lukewarm stew, that seemed, from the frequency of its repetition, to constitute the pride of his culinary art, was sufficient to take away the girl's appetite.

His small, blue, close-set eyes never met hers squarely. There was a shiftiness of his whole appearance that even found expression in the cat-like manner of his gait, and to it all a sinister suggestion was added by the long slim knife that always rested at his waist, slipped through the greasy cord that supported his soiled apron. Ostensibly it was but an implement of his calling; but the girl could never free herself of the conviction that it would require little provocation to witness it put to other and less harmless uses.

His manner toward her was surly, yet she never failed to meet him with a pleasant smile and a word of thanks when he brought her food to her, though more often than not she hurled the bulk of it through the tiny cabin port the moment that the door closed behind him.

During the days of anguish that followed Jane Clayton's imprisonment, but two questions were uppermost in her mind —the whereabouts of her husband and her son. She fully believed that the baby was aboard the *Kincaid*, provided that he still lived, but whether Tarzan had been permitted to live after having been lured aboard the evil craft she could not guess.

She knew, of course, the deep hatred that the Russian felt for the Englishman, and she could think of but one reason for having him brought aboard the ship—to dispatch him in comparative safety in revenge for his having thwarted Rokoff's pet schemes, and for having been at last the means of landing him in a French prison.

Tarzan, on his part, lay in the darkness of his cell, ignorant of the fact that his wife was a prisoner in the cabin almost above his head.

The same Swede that served Jane brought his meals to him, but, though on several occasions Tarzan had tried to draw the man into conversation, he had been unsuccessful.

He had hoped to learn through this fellow whether his little son was aboard the *Kincaid*, but to every question upon this or kindred subjects the fellow returned but one reply, "Ay tank it blow purty soon purty hard." So after several attempts Tarzan gave it up.

For weeks that seemed months to the two prisoners the little steamer forged on they knew not where. Once the *Kincaid* stopped to coal, only immediately to take up the seemingly interminable voyage.

Rokoff had visited Jane Clayton but once since he had locked her in the tiny cabin. He had come gaunt and hollow-eyed from a long siege of sea-sickness. The object of his visit was to obtain from her her personal cheque for a large sum in return for a guarantee of her personal safety and return to England.

"When you set me down safely in any civilized port, together with my son and my husband," she replied, "I will pay you in gold twice the amount you ask; but until then you shall not have a cent, nor the promise of a cent under any other conditions."

"You will give me the cheque I ask," he replied with a snarl, "or neither you nor your child nor your husband will ever again set foot within any port, civilized or otherwise."

"I would not trust you," she replied. "What guarantee have I that you would not take my money and then do as you pleased with me and mine regardless of your promise?"

"I think you will do as I bid," he said, turning to leave the cabin. "Remember that I have your son—if you chance to hear the agonized wail of a tortured child it may console you to reflect that it is because of your stubbornness that the baby suffers—and that it is your baby."

"You would not do it!" cried the girl. "You would not—could not be so fiendishly cruel!"

"It is not I that am cruel, but you," he returned, "for you

permit a paltry sum of money to stand between your baby and immunity from suffering."

The end of it was that Jane Clayton wrote out a cheque of large denomination and handed it to Nikolas Rokoff, who left her cabin with a grin of satisfaction upon his lips.

The following day the hatch was removed from Tarzan's cell, and as he looked up he saw Paulvitch's head framed in the square of light above him.

"Come up," commanded the Russian. "But bear in mind that you will be shot if you make a single move to attack me or any other aboard the ship."

The ape-man swung himself lightly to the deck. About him, but at a respectful distance, stood a half-dozen sailors armed with rifles and revolvers. Facing him was Paulvitch.

Tarzan looked about for Rokoff, who he felt sure must be aboard, but there was no sign of him.

"Lord Greystoke," commenced the Russian, "by your continued and wanton interference with M. Rokoff and his plans you have at last brought yourself and your family to this unfortunate extremity. You have only yourself to thank. As you may imagine, it has cost M. Rokoff a large amount of money to finance this expedition, and, as you are the sole cause of it, he naturally looks to you for reimbursement.

"Further, I may say that only by meeting M. Rokoff's just demands may you avert the most unpleasant consequences to your wife and child, and at the same time retain your own life and regain your liberty."

"What is the amount?" asked Tarzan. "And what assurance have I that you will live up to your end of the agreement? I have little reason to trust two such scoundrels as you and Rokoff, you know."

The Russian flushed.

"You are in no position to deliver insults," he said. "You have no assurance that we will live up to our agreement other than my word, but you have before you the assurance that we can make short work of you if you do not write out the cheque we demand.

"Unless you are a greater fool than I imagine, you should know that there is nothing that would give us greater pleasure than to order these men to fire. That we do not is because we have other plans for punishing you that would be entirely upset by your death."

"Answer one question," said Tarzan. "Is my son on board this ship?"

"No," replied Alexis Paulvitch, "your son is quite safe elsewhere; nor will he be killed until you refuse to accede to our fair demands. If it becomes necessary to kill you, there will be no reason for not killing the child, since with you gone the one whom we wish to punish through the boy will be gone, and he will then be to us only a constant source of danger and embarrassment. You see, therefore, that you may only save the life of your son by saving your own, and you can only save your own by giving us the cheque we ask."

"Very well," replied Tarzan, for he knew that he could trust them to carry out any sinister threat that Paulvitch had made, and there was a bare chance that by conceding their demands he might save the boy.

That they would permit him to live after he had appended his name to the cheque never occurred to him as being within the realms of probability. But he was determined to give them such a battle as they would never forget, and possibly to take Paulvitch with him into eternity. He was only sorry that it was not Rokoff.

He took his pocket cheque-book and fountain-pen from his pocket.

"What is the amount?" he asked.

Paulvitch named an enormous sum. Tarzan could scarce restrain a smile.

Their very cupidity was to prove the means of their undoing, in the matter of the ransom at least. Purposely he hesitated and haggled over the amount, but Paulvitch was obdurate. Finally the ape-man wrote out his cheque for a larger sum than stood to his credit at the bank.

As he turned to hand the worthless slip of paper to the Russian his glance chanced to pass across the starboard bow of the *Kincaid*. To his surprise he saw that the ship lay within a few hundred yards of land. Almost down to the water's edge ran a dense tropical jungle, and behind was higher land clothed in forest.

Paulvitch noted the direction of his gaze.

"You are to be set at liberty here," he said.

Tarzan's plan for immediate physical revenge upon the Russian vanished. He thought the land before him the mainland of Africa, and he knew that should they liberate him here he could doubtless find his way to civilization with comparative ease.

Paulvitch took the cheque.

"Remove your clothing," he said to the ape-man. "Here you will need it."

Tarzan demurred.

Paulvitch pointed to the armed sailors. Then the Englishman slowly divested himself of his clothing.

A boat was lowered, and, still heavily guarded, the ape-man was rowed ashore. Half an hour later the sailors had returned to the *Kincaid,* and the steamer was slowly getting under way.

As Tarzan stood upon the narrow strip of beach watching the departure of the vessel he saw a figure appear at the rail and call aloud to attract his attention.

The ape-man had been about to read a note that one of the sailors had handed him as the small boat that bore him to the shore was on the point of returning to the steamer, but at the hail from the vessel's deck he looked up.

He saw a black-bearded man who laughed at him in derision as he held high above his head the figure of a little child. Tarzan half started as though to rush through the surf and strike out for the already moving steamer; but realizing the futility of so rash an act he halted at the water's edge.

Thus he stood, his gaze riveted upon the *Kincaid* until it disappeared beyond a projecting promontory of the coast.

From the jungle at his back fierce bloodshot eyes glared from beneath shaggy overhanging brows upon him.

Little monkeys in the tree-tops chattered and scolded, and from the distance of the inland forest came the scream of a leopard.

But still John Clayton, Lord Greystoke, stood deaf and unseeing, suffering the pangs of keen regret for the opportunity that he had wasted because he had been so gullible as to place credence in a single statement of the first lieutenant of his arch-enemy.

"I have at least," he thought, "one consolation—the knowledge that Jane is safe in London. Thank Heaven she, too, did not fall into the clutches of those villains."

Behim him the hairy thing whose evil eyes had been watching his as a cat watches a mouse was creeping stealthily toward him.

Where were the trained senses of the savage ape-man? Where the acute hearing?

Where the uncanny sense of scent?

3

SLOWLY Tarzan unfolded the note the sailor had thrust into his hand, and read it. At first it made little impression on his sorrow-numbed senses, but finally the full purport of the hideous plot of revenge unfolded itself before his imagination.

"This will explain to you" [the note read] "the exact nature of my intentions relative to your offspring and to you.

"You were born an ape. You lived naked in the jungles— to your own we have returned you; but your son shall rise a step above his sire. It is the immutable law of evolution.

"The father was a beast, but the son shall be a man—he shall take the next ascending step in the scale of progress. He shall be no naked beast of the jungle, but shall wear a loin-cloth and copper anklets, and, perchance, a ring in his nose, for he is to be reared by men—a tribe of savage cannibals.

"I might have killed you, but that would have curtailed the full measure of the punishment you have earned at my hands.

"Dead, you could not have suffered in the knowledge of your son's plight; but living and in a place from which you may not escape to seek or succour your child, you shall suffer worse than death for all the years of your life in contemplation of the horrors of your son's existence.

"This, then, is to be a part of your punishment for having dared to pit yourself against   N. R.

"P.S.—The balance of your punishment has to do with what shall presently befall your wife—that I shall leave to your imagination."

As he finished reading, a slight sound behind him brought him back with a start to the world of present realities.

Instantly his senses awoke, and he was again Tarzan of the Apes.

As he wheeled about, it was a beast at bay, vibrant with the instinct of self-preservation, that faced a huge bull-ape that was already charging down upon him.

The two years that had elapsed since Tarzan had come out of the savage forest with his rescued mate had witnessed slight diminution of the mighty powers that had made him the invincible lord of the jungle. His great estates in Uziri had claimed much of his time and attention, and there he had found ample field for the practical use and retention of his almost superhuman powers; but naked and unarmed to do battle with the shaggy, bull-necked beast that now confronted him was a test that the ape-man would scarce have welcomed at any period of his wild existence.

But there was no alternative other than to meet the rage-maddened creature with the weapons with which nature had endowed him.

Over the bull's shoulder Tarzan could see now the heads and shoulder of perhaps a dozen more of these mighty forerunners of primitive man.

He knew, however, that there was little chance that they would attack him, since it is not within the reasoning powers of the anthropoid to be able to weigh or appreciate the value of concentrated action against an enemy—otherwise they would long since have become the dominant creatures of their haunts, so tremendous a power of destruction lies in their mighty thews and savage fangs.

With a low snarl the beast now hurled himself at Tarzan, but the ape-man had found, among other things in the haunts of civilized man, certain methods of scientific warfare that are unknown to the jungle folk.

Whereas, a few years since, he would have met the brute rush with brute force, he now sidestepped his antagonist's headlong charge, and as the brute hurtled past him swung a mighty right to the pit of the ape's stomach.

With a howl of mingled rage and anguish the great anthropoid bent double and sank to the ground, though almost instantly he was again struggling to his feet.

Before he could regain them, however, his white-skinned foe had wheeled and pounced upon him, and in the act there dropped from the shoulders of the English lord the last shred of his superficial mantle of civilization.

Once again he was the jungle beast revelling in bloody

conflict with his kind. Once again he was Tarzan, son of Kala the she-ape.

His strong, white teeth sank into the hairy throat of his enemy as he sought the pulsing jugular.

Powerful fingers held the mighty fangs from his own flesh, or clenched and beat with the power of a steam-hammer upon the snarling, foam-flecked face of his adversary.

In a circle about them the balance of the tribe of apes stood watching and enjoying the struggle. They muttered low gutturals of approval as bits of white hide or hairy bloodstained skin were torn from one contestant or the other. But they were silent in amazement and expectation when they saw the mighty white ape wriggle upon the back of their king, and, with steel muscles tensed beneath the armpits of his antagonist, bear down mightily with his open palms upon the back of the thick bullneck, so that the king ape could but shriek in agony and flounder helplessly about upon the thick mat of jungle grass.

As Tarzan had overcome the huge Terkoz that time years before when he had been about to set out upon his quest for human beings of his own kind and colour, so now he overcame this other great ape with the same wrestling hold upon which he had stumbled by accident during that other combat.

The little audience of fierce anthropoids heard the creaking of their king's neck mingling with his agonized shrieks and hideous roaring.

Then there came a sudden crack, like the breaking of a stout limb before the fury of the wind. The bullet-head crumpled forward upon its flaccid neck against the great hairy chest—the roaring and the shrieking ceased.

The little pig-eyes of the onlookers wandered from the still form of their leader to that of the white ape that was rising to its feet beside the vanquished, then back to their king as though in wonder that he did not arise and slay this presumptuous stranger.

They saw the new-comer place a foot upon the neck of the quiet figure at his feet and, throwing back his head, give vent to the wild, uncanny challenge of the bull-ape that has made a kill. Then they knew that their king was dead.

Across the jungle rolled the horrid notes of the victory cry. The little monkeys in the tree-tops ceased their chattering. The harsh-voiced, brilliant-plumed birds were still. From afar came the answering wail of a leopard and the deep roar of a lion.

It was the old Tarzan who turned questioning eyes upon the little knot of apes before him. It was the old Tarzan who

shook his head as though to toss back a heavy mane that
had fallen before his face—an old habit dating from the days
that his great shock of thick, black hair had fallen about his
shoulders, and often tumbled before his eyes when it had
meant life or death to him to have his vision unobstructed.

The ape-man knew that he might expect an immediate
attack on the part of that particular surviving bull-ape who
felt himself best fitted to contend for the kingship of the
tribe. Among his own apes he knew that it was not unusual
for an entire stranger to enter a community and, after having
dispatched the king, assume the leadership of the tribe himself, together with the fallen monarch's mates.

On the other hand, if he made no attempt to follow them,
they might move slowly away from him, later to fight among
themselves for the supremacy. That he could be king of
them, if he so chose, he was confident; but he was not sure
he cared to assume the sometimes irksome duties of that
position, for he could see no particular advantage to be
gained thereby.

One of the younger apes, a huge, splendidly muscled
brute, was edging threateningly closer to the ape-man.
Through his bared fighting fangs there issued a low, sullen
growl.

Tarzan watched his every move, standing rigid as a
statue. To have fallen back a step would have been to pre-
cipitate an immediate charge; to have rushed forward to
meet the other might have had the same result, or it might
have put the bellicose one to flight—it all depended upon
the young bull's stock of courage.

To stand perfectly still, waiting, was the middle course.
In this event the bull would, according to custom, approach
quite close to the object of his attention, growling hideously
and baring slavering fangs. Slowly he would circle about the
other, as though with a chip upon his shoulder; and this he
did, even as Tarzan had foreseen.

It might be a bluff royal, or, on the other hand, so un-
stable is the mind of an ape, a passing impulse might hurl
the hairy mass, tearing and rending, upon the man without
an instant's warning.

As the brute circled him Tarzan turned slowly, keeping
his eyes ever upon the eyes of his antagonist. He had ap-
praised the young bull as one who had never quite felt equal
to the task of overthrowing his former king, but who one day
would have done so. Tarzan saw that the beast was of
wondrous proportions, standing over seven feet upon his
short, bowed legs.

His great, hairy arms reached almost to the ground even when he stood erect, and his fighting fangs, now quite close to Tarzan's face, were exceptionally long and sharp. Like the others of his tribe, he differed in several minor essentials from the apes of Tarzan's boyhood.

At first the ape-man had experienced a thrill of hope at sight of the shaggy bodies of the anthropoids—a hope that by some strange freak of fate he had been again returned to his own tribe; but a closer inspection had convinced him that these were of another species.

As the threatening bull continued his stiff and jerky circling of the ape-man, much after the manner that you have noted among dogs when a strange canine comes among them, it occurred to Tarzan to discover if the language of his own tribe was identical with that of this other family, and so he addressed the brute in the language of the tribe of Kerchak.

"Who are you," he asked, "who threatens Tarzan of the Apes?"

The hairy brute looked his surprise.

"I am Akut," replied the other in the same simple, primal tongue which is so low in the scale of spoken languages that, as Tarzan had surmised, it was identical with that of the tribe in which the first twenty years of his life had been spent.

"I am Akut," said the ape. "Molak is dead. I am king. Go away or I shall kill you!"

"You saw how easily I killed Mokak," replied Tarzan. "So could I kill you if I cared to be king. But Tarzan of the Apes would not be king of the tribe of Akut. All he wishes is to live in peace in this country. Let us be friends. Tarzan of the Apes can help you, and you can help Tarzan of the Apes."

"You cannot kill Akut," replied the other. "None is so great as Akut. Had you not killed Molak, Akut would have done so, for Akut was ready to be king."

For answer the ape-man hurled himself upon the great brute who during the conversation had slightly relaxed his vigilance.

In the twinkling of an eye the man had seized the wrist of the great ape, and before the other could grapple with him had whirled him about and leaped upon his broad back.

Down they went together, but so well had Tarzan's plan worked out that before ever they touched the ground he had gained the same hold upon Akut that had broken Molak's neck.

Slowly he brought the pressure to bear, and then as in

days gone by he had given Kerchak the chance to surrender
and live, so now he gave to Akut—in whom he saw a
possible ally of great strength and resource—the option of
living in amity with him or dying as he had just seen his
savage and heretofore invincible king die.

"*Ka-goda?*" whispered Tarzan to the ape beneath him.

It was the same question that he had whispered to Kerchak, and in the language of the apes it means, broadly,
"Do you surrender?"

Akut thought of the creaking sound he had heard just
before Molak's thick neck had snapped, and he shuddered.

He hated to give up the kingship, though, so again he
struggled to free himself; but a sudden torturing pressure
upon his vertebra brought an agonized "*ka-goda!*" from his
lips.

Tarzan relaxed his grip a trifle.

"You may still be king, Akut," he said. "Tarzan told you
that he did not wish to be king. If any question your right,
Tarzan of the Apes will help you in your battles."

The ape-man rose, and Akut came slowly to his feet.
Shaking his bullet head and growling angrily, he waddled
toward his tribe, looking first at one and then at another of
the larger bulls who might be expected to challenge his
leadership.

But none did so; instead, they drew away as he approached, and presently the whole pack moved off into the
jungle, and Tarzan was left alone once more upon the beach.

The ape-man was sore from the wounds that Molak had
inflicted upon him, but he was inured to physical suffering
and endured it with the calm and fortitude of the wild beasts
that had taught him to lead the jungle life after the manner
of all those that are born to it.

His first need, he realized, was for weapons of offence
and defence, for his encounter with the apes, and the distant
notes of the savage voices of Numa the lion, and Sheeta, the
panther, warned him that his was to be no life of indolent
ease and security.

It was but a return to the old existence of constant blood-
shed and danger—to the hunting and the being hunted. Grim
beasts would stalk him, as they had stalked him in the past,
and never would there be a moment, by savage day or by
cruel night, that he might not have instant need of such
crude weapons as he could fashion from the materials at
hand.

Upon the shore he found an out-cropping of brittle,
igneous rock. By dint of much labour he managed to chip

off a narrow sliver some twelve inches long by a quarter of an inch thick. One edge was quite thin for a few inches near the tip. It was the rudiment of a knife.

With it he went into the jungle, searching until he found a fallen tree of a certain species of hardwood with which he was familiar. From this he cut a small straight branch, which he pointed at one end.

Then he scooped a small, round hole in the surface of the prostrate trunk. Into this he crumbled a few bits of dry bark, minutely shredded, after which he inserted the tip of his pointed stick, and, sitting astride the bole of the tree, spun the slender rod rapidly between his palms.

After a time a thin smoke rose from the little mass of tinder, and a moment later the whole broke into flame. Heaping some larger twigs and sticks upon the tiny fire, Tarzan soon had quite a respectable blaze roaring in the enlarging cavity of the dead tree.

Into this he thrust the blade of his stone knife, and as it became superheated he would withdraw it, touching a spot near the thin edge with a drop of moisture. Beneath the wetted area a little flake of the glassy material would crack and scale away.

Thus, very slowly, the ape-man commenced the tedious operation of putting a thin edge upon his primitive hunting-knife.

He did not attempt to accomplish the feat all in one sitting. At first he was content to achieve a cutting edge of a couple of inches, with which he cut a long, pliable bow, a handle for his knife, a stout cudgel, and a goodly supply of arrows.

These he cached in a tall tree beside a little stream, and here also he constructed a platform with a roof of palm-leaves above it.

When all these things had been finished it was growing dusk, and Tarzan felt a strong desire to eat.

H had noted during the brief incursion he had made into the forest that a short distance up-stream from his tree there was a much-used watering place, where, from the trampled mud of either bank, it was evident beasts of all sorts and in great numbers came to drink. To this spot the hungry ape-man made his silent way.

Through the upper terrace of the tree-tops he swung with the grace and ease of a monkey. But for the heavy burden upon his heart he would have been happy in this return to the old free life of his boyhood.

Yet even with that burden he fell into the little habits

and manners of his early life that were in reality more a part of him than the thin veneer of civilization that the past three years of his association with the white men of the outer world had spread lightly over him—a veneer that only hid the crudities of the beast that Tarzan of the Apes had been.

Could his fellow-peers of the House of Lords have seen him then they would have held up their noble hands in holy horror.

Silently he crouched in the lower branches of a great forest giant that overhung the trail, his keen eyes and sensitive ears strained into the distant jungle, from which he knew his dinner would presently emerge.

Nor had he long to wait.

Scarce had he settled himself to a comfortable position, his lithe, muscular legs drawn well up beneath him as the panther draws his hindquarters in preparation for the spring, than Bara, the deer, came daintily down to drink.

But more than Bara was coming. Behind the graceful buck came another which the deer could neither see nor scent, but whose movements were apparent to Tarzan of the Apes because of the elevated position of the ape-man's ambush.

He knew not yet exactly the nature of the thing that moved so stealthily through the jungle a few hundred yards behind the deer; but he was convinced that it was some great beast of prey stalking Bara for the selfsame purpose as that which prompted him to await the fleet animal. Numa, perhaps, or Sheeta, the panther.

In any event, Tarzan could see his repast slipping from his grasp unless Bara moved more rapidly toward the ford than at present.

Even as these thoughts passed through his mind some noise of the stalker in his rear must have come to the buck, for with a sudden start he paused for an instant, trembling, in his tracks, and then with a swift bound dashed straight for the river and Tarzan. It was his intention to flee through the shallow ford and escape upon the opposite side of the river.

Not a hundred yards behind him came Numa.

Tarzan could see him quite plainly now. Below the ape-man Bara was about to pass. Could he do it? But even as he asked himself the question the hungry man launched himself from his perch full upon the back of the startled buck.

In another instant Numa would be upon them both, so if

the ape-man were to dine that night, or ever again, he must act quickly.

Scarcely had he touched the sleek hide of the deer with a momentum that sent the animal to its knees than he had grasped a horn in either hand, and with a single quick wrench twisted the animal's neck completely round, until he felt the vertebrae snap beneath his grip.

The lion was roaring in rage close behind him as he swung the deer across his shoulder, and, grasping a foreleg between his strong teeth, leaped for the nearest of the lower branches that swung above his head.

With both hands he grasped the limb, and, at the instant that Numa sprang, drew himself and his prey out of reach of the animal's cruel talons.

There was a thud below him as the baffled cat fell back to earth, and then Tarzan of the Apes, drawing his dinner farther up to the safety of a higher limb, looked down with grinning face into the gleaming yellow eyes of the other wild beast that glared up at him from beneath, and with taunting insults flaunted the tender carcass of his kill in the face of him whom he had cheated of it.

With his crude stone knife he cut a juicy steak from the hindquarters, and while the great lion paced, growling, back and forth below him, Lord Greystoke filled his savage belly, nor ever in the choicest of his exclusive London clubs had a meal tasted more palatable.

The warm blood of his kill smeared his hands and face and filled his nostrils with the scent that the savage carnivora love best.

And when he had finished he left the balance of the carcass in a high fork of the tree where he had dined, and with Numa trailing below him, still keen for revenge, he made his way back to his tree-top shelter, where he slept until the sun was high the following morning.

4

Sheeta

THE next few days were occupied by Tarzan in completing his weapons and exploring the jungle. He strung his bow with tendons from the buck upon which he had dined his first evening upon the new shore, and though he would have preferred the gut of Sheeta for the purpose, he was content to wait until opportunity permitted him to kill one of the great cats.

He also braided a long grass rope—such a rope as he had used so many years before to tantalize the ill-natured Tublat, and which later had developed into a wondrous effective weapon in the practised hands of the little ape-boy.

A sheath and handle for his hunting-knife he fashioned, and a quiver for arrows, and from the hide of Bara a belt and loin-cloth. Then he set out to learn something of the strange land in which he found himself. That it was not his old familiar west coast of the African continent he knew from the fact that it faced east—the rising sun came up out of the sea before the threshold of the jungle.

But that it was not the east coast of Africa he was equally positive, for he felt satisfied that the *Kincaid* had not passed through the Mediterranean, the Suez Canal, and the Red Sea, nor had she had time to round the Cape of Good Hope. So he was quite at a loss to know where he might be.

Sometimes he wondered if the ship had crossed the broad Atlantic to deposit him upon some wild South American shore; but the presence of Numa, the lion, decided him that such could not be the case.

As Tarzan made his lonely way through the jungle paralleling the shore, he felt strong upon him a desire for companionship, so that gradually he commenced to regret that he had not cast his lot with the apes. He had seen nothing

30

of them since that first day, when the influences of civilization were still paramount within him.

Now he was more nearly returned to the Tarzan of old, and though he appreciated the fact that there could be little in common between himself and the great anthropoids, still they were better than no company at all.

Moving leisurely, sometimes upon the ground and again among the lower branches of the trees, gathering an occasional fruit or turning over a fallen log in search of the larger bugs, which he still found as palatable as of old, Tarzan had covered a mile or more when his attention was attracted by the scent of Sheeta up-wind ahead of him.

Now Sheeta, the panther, was one whom Tarzan was exceptionally glad to fall in with, for he had it in mind not only to utilize the great cat's strong gut for his bow, but also to fashion a new quiver and loin-cloth from pieces of his hide. So, whereas the ape-man had gone carelessly before, he now became the personification of noiseless stealth.

Swiftly and silently he glided through the forest in the wake of the savage cat, nor was the pursuer, for all his noble birth, one whit less savage than the wild, fierce thing he stalked.

As he came closer to Sheeta he became aware that the panther on his part was stalking game of his own, and even as he realized this fact there came to his nostrils, wafted from his right by a vagrant breeze, the strong odour of a company of great apes.

The panther had taken to a large tree as Tarzan came within sight of him, and beyond and below him Tarzan saw the tribe of Akut lolling in a little, natural clearing. Some of them were dozing against the boles of trees, while others roamed about turning over bits of bark from beneath which they transferred the luscious grubs and beetles to their mouths.

Akut was the closest to Sheeta.

The great cat lay crouched upon a thick limb, hidden from the ape's view by dense foliage, waiting patiently until the anthropoid should come within range of his spring.

Tarzan cautiously gained a position in the same tree with the panther and a little above him. In his left hand he grasped his slim stone blade. He would have preferred to use his noose, but the foliage surrounding the huge cat precluded the possibility of an accurate throw with the rope.

Akut had now wandered quite close beneath the tree wherein lay the waiting death. Sheeta slowly edged his hind paws along the branch still further beneath him, and then with a hideous shriek he launched himself toward the great ape. The barest fraction of a second before his spring another beast of prey above him leaped, its weird and savage cry mingling with his.

As the startled Akut looked up he saw the panther almost above him, and already upon the panther's back the white ape that had bested him that day near the great water.

The teeth of the ape-man were buried in the back of Sheeta's neck and his right arm was round the fierce throat, while the left hand, grasping a slender piece of stone, rose and fell in mighty blows upon the panther's side behind the left shoulder.

Akut had just time to leap to one side to avoid being pinioned beneath these battling monsters of the jungle.

With a crash they came to earth at his feet. Sheeta was screaming, snarling, and roaring horribly; but the white ape clung tenaciously and in silence to the thrashing body of his quarry.

Steadily and remorselessly the stone knife was driven home through the glossy hide—time and again it drank deep, until with a final agonized lunge and shriek the great feline rolled over upon its side and, save for the spasmodic jerking of its muscles, lay quiet and still in death.

Then the ape-man raised his head, as he stood over the carcass of his kill, and once again through the jungle rang his wild and savage victory challenge.

Akut and the apes of Akut stood looking in startled wonder at the dead body of Sheeta and the lithe, straight figure of the man who had slain him.

Tarzan was the first to speak.

He had saved Akut's life for a purpose, and, knowing the limitations of the ape intellect, he also knew that he must make this purpose plain to the anthropoid if it were to serve him in the way he hoped.

"I am Tarzan of the Apes," he said, "Mighty hunter. Mighty fighter. By the great water I spared Akut's life when I might have taken it and become king of the tribe of Akut. Now I have saved Akut from death beneath the rending fangs of Sheeta.

"When Akut or the tribe of Akut is in danger, let them call to Tarzan thus"—and the ape-man raised the hideous cry with which the tribe of Kerchak had been wont to summon its absent members in times of peril.

"And," he continued, "when they hear Tarzan call to them, let them remember what he has done for Akut and come to him with great speed. Shall it be as Tarzan says?"

"*Huh!*" assented Akut, and from the members of his tribe there rose a unanimous "*Huh.*"

Then, presently, they went to feeding again as though nothing had happened, and with them fed John Clayton, Lord Greystoke.

He noticed, however, that Akut kept always close to him, and was often looking at him with a strange wonder in his little bloodshot eyes, and once he did a thing that Tarzan during all his long years among the apes had never before seen an ape do—he found a particularly tender morsel and handed it to Tarzan.

As the tribe hunted, the glistening body of the ape-man mingled with the brown, shaggy hides of his companions. Oftentimes they brushed together in passing, but the apes had already taken his presence for granted, so that he was as much one of them as Akut himself.

If he came too close to a she with a young baby, the former would bare her great fighting fangs and growl ominously, and occasionally a truculent young bull would snarl a warning if Tarzan approached while the former was eating. But in these things the treatment was no different from that which they accorded any other member of the tribe.

Tarzan on his part felt very much at home with these fierce, hairy progenitors of primitive man. He skipped nimbly out of reach of each threatening female—for such is the way of apes, if they be not in one of their occasional fits of bestial rage—and he growled back at the truculent young bulls, baring his canine teeth even as they. Thus easily he fell back into the way of his early life, nor did it seem that he had ever tasted association with creatures of his own kind.

For the better part of a week he roamed the jungle with his new friends, partly because of a desire for companionship and partially through a well-laid plan to impress himself indelibly upon their memories, which at best are none too long; for Tarzan from past experience knew that it might serve him in good stead to have a tribe of these powerful and terrible beasts at his call.

When he was convinced that he had succeeded to some extent in fixing his identity upon them he decided to again take up his exploration. To this end he set out toward the north early one day, and, keeping parallel with the shore, travelled rapidly until amost nightfall.

When the sun rose the next morning he saw that it lay almost directly to his right as he stood upon the beach instead of straight out across the water as heretofore, and so he reasoned that the shore line had trended toward the west. All the second day he continued his rapid course, and when Tarzan of the Apes sought speed, he passed through the middle terrace of the forest with the rapidity of a squirrel.

That night the sun set straight out across the water opposite the land, and then the ape-man guessed at last the truth that he had been suspecting.

Rokoff had set him ashore upon an island.

He might have known it! If there was any plan that would render his position more harrowing he should have known that such would be the one adopted by the Russian, and what could be more terrible that to leave him to a lifetime of suspense upon an uninhabited island?

Rokoff doubtless had sailed directly to the mainland, where it would be a comparatively easy thing for him to find the means of delivering the infant Jack into the hands of the cruel and savage foster-parents, who, as his note had threatened, would have the upbringing of the child.

Tarzan shuddered as he thought of the cruel suffering the little one must endure in such a life, even though he might fall into the hands of individuals whose intentions toward him were of the kindest. The ape-man had had sufficient experience with the lower savages of Africa to know that even there may be found the cruder virtues of charity and humanity; but their lives were at best but a series of terrible privations, dangers, and sufferings.

Then there was the horrid after-fate that awaited the child as he grew to manhood. The horrible practices that would form a part of his life-training would alone be sufficient to bar him forever from association with those of his own race and station in life.

A cannibal! His little boy a savage man-eater! It was too horrible to contemplate.

The filed teeth, the slit nose, the little face painted hideously.

Tarzan groaned. Could he but feel the throat of the Russ fiend beneath his steel fingers!

And Jane!

What tortures of doubt and fear and uncertainty she must be suffering. He felt that his position was infinitely less terrible than hers, for he at least knew that one of his loved ones was safe at home, while she had no idea of the whereabouts of either her husband or her son.

It is well for Tarzan that he did not guess the truth, for

the knowledge would have but added a hundredfold to his suffering.

As he moved slowly through the jungle, his mind absorbed by his gloomy thoughts, there presently came to his ears a strange scratching sound which he could not translate.

Cautiously he moved in the direction from which it emanated, presently coming upon a huge panther pinned beneath a fallen tree.

As Tarzan approached the beast turned, snarling, toward him, struggling to extricate itself; but one great limb across its back and the smaller entangling branches pinioning its legs prevented it from moving but a few inches in any direction.

The ape-man stood before the helpless cat fitting an arrow to his bow that he might dispatch the beast that otherwise must die of starvation; but even as he drew back the shaft a sudden whim stayed his hand.

Why rob the poor creature of life and liberty, when it would be so easy a thing to restore both to it! He was sure from the fact that the panther moved all its limbs in its futile struggle for freedom that its spine was uninjured, and for the same reason he knew that none of its limbs were broken.

Relaxing his bowstring, he returned the arrow to the quiver and, throwing the bow about his shoulder, stepped closer to the pinioned beast.

On his lips was the soothing, purring sound that the great cats themselves make when contented and happy. It was the nearest approach to a friendly advance that Tarzan could make in the language of Sheeta.

The panther ceased his snarling and eyed the ape-man closely. To lift the tree's great weight from the animal it was necessary to come within reach of those long, strong talons, and when the tree had been removed the man would be totally at the mercy of the savage beast; but to Tarzan of the Apes fear was a thing unknown.

Having decided, he acted promptly.

Unhesitatingly, he stepped into the tangle of branches close to the panther's side, still voicing his friendly and conciliatory purr. The cat turned his head toward the man, eyeing him steadily—questioningly. The long fangs were bared, but more in preparedness than threat.

Tarzan put a broad shoulder beneath the bole of the tree, and as he did so his bare leg pressed against the cat's silken side, so close was the man to the great beast.

Slowly Tarzan extended his giant thews.

The great tree with its entangling branches rose gradually from the panther, who, feeling the encumbering weight diminish, quickly crawled from beneath. Tarzan let the tree fall back to earth, and the two beasts turned to look upon one another.

A grim smile lay upon the ape-man's lips, for he knew that he had taken his life in his hands to free this savage jungle fellow; nor would it have surprised him had the cat sprung upon him the instant that it had been released.

But it did not do so. Instead, it stood a few paces from the tree watching the ape-man clamber out of the maze of fallen branches.

Once outside, Tarzan was not three paces from the panther. He might have taken to the higher branches of the trees upon the opposite side, for Sheeta cannot climb to the heights to which the ape-man can go; but something, a spirit of bravado perhaps, prompted him to approach the panther as though to discover if any feeling of gratitude would prompt the beast to friendliness.

As he approached the mighty cat the creature stepped warily to one side, and the ape-man brushed past him within a foot of the dripping jaws, and as he continued on through the forest the panther followed on behind him, as a hound follows at heel.

For a long time Tarzan could not tell whether the beast was following out of friendly feelings or merely stalking him against the time he should be hungry; but finally he was forced to believe that the former incentive it was that prompted the animal's action.

Later in the day the scent of a deer sent Tarzan into the trees, and when he had dropped his noose about the animal's neck he called to Sheeta, using a purr similar to that which he had utilized to pacify the brute's suspicions earlier in the day, but a trifle louder and more shrill.

It was similar to that which he had heard panthers use after a kill when they had been hunting in pairs.

Almost immediately there was a crashing of the underbrush close at hand, and the long, lithe body of his strange companion broke into view.

At sight of the body of Bara and the smell of blood the panther gave forth a shrill scream, and a moment later two beasts were feeding side by side upon the tender meat of the deer.

For several days this strangely assorted pair roamed the jungle together.

When one made a kill he called the other, and thus they fed well and often.

On one occasion as they were dining upon the carcass of a boar that Sheeta had dispatched, Numa, the lion, grim and terrible, broke through the tangled grasses close beside them.

With an angry, warning roar he sprang forward to chase them from their kill. Sheeta bounded into a near-by thicket, while Tarzan took to the low branches of an overhanging tree.

Here the ape-man unloosed his grass rope from about his neck, and as Numa stood above the body of the boar, challenging head erect, he dropped the sinuous noose about the maned neck, drawing the stout strands taut with a sudden jerk. At the same time he called shrilly to Sheeta, as he drew the struggling lion upward until only his hind feet touched the ground.

Quickly he made the rope fast to a stout branch, and as the panther, in answer to his summons, leaped into sight, Tarzan dropped to the earth beside the struggling and infuriated Numa, and with long, sharp knife sprang upon him at one side even as Sheeta did upon the other.

The panther tore and rent Numa upon the right, while the ape-man struck home with his stone knife upon the other, so that before the mighty clawing of the king of beasts had succeeded in parting the rope he hung quite dead and harmless in the noose.

And then upon the jungle air there rose in unison from two savage throats the victory cry of the bull ape and the panther, blended into one frightful and uncanny scream.

As the last notes died away in a long-drawn, fearsome wail, a score of painted warriors, drawing their long warcanoe upon the beach, halted to stare in the direction of the jungle and to listen.

5

Mugambi

B Y the time that Tarzan had travelled entirely about the coast of the island, and made several trips inland from various points, he was sure that he was the only human being upon it.

Nowhere had he found any sign that men had stopped even temporarily upon this shore, though, of course, he knew that so quickly does the rank vegetation of the tropics erase all but the most permanent of human monuments that he might be in error in his deductions.

The day following the killing of Numa, Tarzan and Sheeta came upon the tribe of Akut. At sight of the panther the great apes took to flight, but after a time Tarzan succeeded in recalling them.

It had occurred to him that it would be at least an interesting experiment to attempt to reconcile these hereditary enemies. He welcomed anything that would occupy his time and his mind beyond the filling of his belly and the gloomy thoughts to which he fell prey the moment that he became idle.

To communicate his plan to the apes was not a particularly difficult matter, though their narrow and limited vocabulary was strained in the effort; but to impress upon the little, wicked brain of Sheeta that he was to hunt with and not for his legitimate prey proved a task almost beyond the powers of the ape-man.

Tarzan, among his other weapons, possessed a long, stout cudgel, and after fastening his rope about the panther's neck he used this instrument freely upon the snarling beast, endeavouring in this way to impress upon its memory that it must not attack the great, shaggy, manlike creatures that had

38

approached more closely once they had seen the purpose of the rope about Sheeta's neck.

That the cat did not turn and rend Tarzan is something of a miracle which may possibly be accounted for by the fact that twice when it turned growling upon the ape-man he had rapped it sharply upon its sensitive nose, inculcating in its mind thereby a most wholesome fear of the cudgel and the ape-beasts behind it.

It is a question if the original cause of his attachment for Tarzan was still at all clear in the mind of the panther, though doubtless some subconscious suggestion, superinduced by this primary reason and aided and abetted by the habit of the past few days, did much to compel the beast to tolerate treatment at his hands that would have sent it at the throat of any other creature.

Then, too, there was the compelling force of the man-mind exerting its powerful influence over this creature of a lower order, and, after all, it may have been this that proved the most potent factor in Tarzan's supremacy over Sheeta and the other beasts of the jungle that had from time to time fallen under his domination.

Be that as it may, for days the man, the panther, and the great apes roamed their savage haunts side by side, making their kills together and sharing them with one another, and of all the fierce and savage band none was more terrible than the smooth-skinned, powerful beast that had been but a few short months before a familiar figure in many a London drawing room.

Sometimes the beasts separated to follow their own inclinations for an hour or a day, and it was upon one of these occasions when the ape-man had wandered through the tree-tops toward the beach, and was stretched in the hot sun upon the sand, that from the low summit of a near-by promontory a pair of keen eyes discovered him.

For a moment the owner of the eyes looked in astonishment at the figure of the savage white man basking in the rays of that hot, tropic sun; then he turned, making a sign to some one behind him. Presently another pair of eyes were looking down upon the ape-man, and then another and another, until a full score of hideously trapped, savage warriors were lying upon their bellies along the crest of the ridge watching the white-skinned stranger.

They were down wind from Tarzan, and so their scent was not carried to him, and as his back was turned half toward them he did not see their cautious advance over the

edge of the promontory and down through the rank grass
toward the sandy beach where he lay.

Big fellows they were, all of them, their barbaric head-
dresses and grotesquely painted faces, together with their
many metal ornaments and gorgeously coloured feathers,
adding to their wild, fierce appearance.

Once at the foot of the ridge, they came cautiously to their
feet, and, bent half-double, advanced silently upon the unconscious white man, their heavy war-clubs swinging men-
acingly in their brawny hands.

The mental suffering that Tarzan's sorrowful thoughts induced had the effect of numbing his keen, perceptive facul-
ties, so that the advancing savages were almost upon him
before he became aware that he was no longer alone upon
the beach.

So quickly, though, were his mind and muscles wont to
react in unison to the slightest alarm that he was upon his
feet and facing his enemies, even as he realized that something was behind him. As he sprang to his feet the warriors
leaped toward him with raised clubs and savage yells, but
the foremost went down to sudden death beneath the long,
stout stick of the ape-man, and then the lithe, sinewy figure
was among them, striking right and left with a fury, power,
and precision that brought panic to the ranks of the blacks.

For a moment they withdrew, those that were left of
them, and consulted together at a short distance from the
ape-man, who stood with folded arms, a half-smile upon his
handsome face, watching them. Presently they advanced
upon him once more, this time wielding their heavy war-
spears. They were between Tarzan and the jungle, in a little
semicircle that closed in upon him as they advanced.

There seemed to the ape-man but slight chance to escape
the final charge when all the great spears should be hurled
simultaneously at him; but if he had desired to escape there
was no way other than through the ranks of the savages
except the open sea behind him.

His predicament was indeed most serious when an idea
occurred to him that altered his smile to a broad grin. The
warriors were still some little distance away, advancing
slowly, making, after the manner of their kind, a frightful
din with their savage yells and the pounding of their naked
feet upon the ground as they leaped up and down in a
fantastic war dance.

Then it was that the ape-man lifted his voice in a series
of wild, weird screams that brought the blacks to a sudden,
perplexed halt. They looked at one another questioningly,

for here was a sound so hideous that their own frightful din faded into insignificance beside it. No human throat could have formed those bestial notes, they were sure, and yet with their own eyes they had seen this white man open his mouth to pour forth his awful cry.

But only for a moment they hesitated, and then with one accord they again took up their fantastic advance upon their prey; but even then a sudden crashing in the jungle behind them brought them once more to a halt, and as they turned to look in the direction of this new noise there broke upon their startled visions a sight that may well have frozen the blood of braver men than the Wagambi.

Leaping from the tangled vegetation of the jungle's rim came a huge panther, with blazing eyes and bared fangs, and in his wake a score of mighty, shaggy apes lumbering rapidly toward them, half erect upon their short, bowed legs, and with their long arms reaching to the ground, where their horny knuckles bore the weight of their ponderous bodies as they lurched from side to side in their grotesque advance.

The beasts of Tarzan had come in answer to his call.

Before the Wagambi could recover from their astonishment the frightful horde was upon them from one side and Tarzan of the Apes from the other. Heavy spears were hurled and mighty war-clubs wielded, and though apes went down never to rise, so, too, went down the men of Ugambi.

Sheeta's cruel fangs and tearing talons ripped and tore at the black hides. Akut's mighty yellow tusks found the jugular of more than one sleek-skinned savage, and Tarzan of the Apes was here and there and everywhere, urging on his fierce allies and taking a heavy toll with his long, slim knife.

In a moment the blacks had scattered for their lives, but of the score that had crept down the grassy sides of the promontory only a single warrior managed to escape the horde that had overwhelmed his people.

This one was Mugambi, chief of the Wagambi of Ugambi, and as he disappeared in the tangled luxuriousness of the rank growth upon the ridge's summit only the keen eyes of the ape-man saw the direction of his flight.

Leaving his pack to eat their fill upon the flesh of their victims—flesh that he could not touch—Tarzan of the Apes pursued the single survivor of the bloody fray. Just beyond the ridge he came within sight of the fleeing black, making with headlong leaps for a long war-canoe that was drawn well up upon the beach above the high tide surf.

Noiseless as the fellow's shadow, the ape-man raced after

the terror-stricken black. In the white man's mind was a new plan, awakened by sight of the war-canoe. If these men had come to his island from another, or from the mainland, why not utilize their craft to make his way to the country from which they had come? Evidently it was an inhabited country, and no doubt had occasional intercourse with the mainland, if it were not itself upon the continent of Africa.

A heavy hand fell upon the shoulder of the escaping Mugambi before he was aware that he was being pursued, and as he turned to do battle with his assailant giant fingers closed about his wrists and he was hurled to earth with a giant astride him before he could strike a blow in his own defence.

In the language of the West Coast, Tarzan spoke to the prostrate man beneath him.

"Who are you?" he asked.

"Mugambi, chief of the Wagambi," replied the black.

"I will spare your life," said Tarzan, "if you will promise to help me to leave this island. What do you answer?"

"I will help you," replied Mugambi. "But now that you have killed all my warriors, I do not know that even I can leave your country, for there will be none to wield the paddles, and without paddlers we cannot cross the water."

Tarzan rose and allowed his prisoner to come to his feet. The fellow was a magnificent specimen of manhood—a black counterpart in physique of the splendid white man whom he faced.

"Come!" said the ape-man, and started back in the direction from which they could hear the snarling and growling of the feasting pack. Mugambi drew back.

"They will kill us," he said.

"I think not," replied Tarzan. "They are mine."

Still the black hesitated, fearful of the consequences of approaching the terrible creatures that were dining upon the bodies of his warriors; but Tarzan forced him to accompany him, and presently the two emerged from the jungle in full view of the grisly spectacle upon the beach. At sight of the men the beasts looked up with menacing growls, but Tarzan strode in among them, dragging the trembling Wagambi with him.

As he had taught the apes to accept Sheeta, so he taught them to adopt Mugambi as well, and much more easily; but Sheeta seemed quite unable to understand that though he had been called upon to devour Mugambi's warriors he was not to be allowed to proceed after the same fashion with Mugambi. However, being well filled, he contented himself with walking round the terror-stricken savage, emitting low, menacing growls the while he kept his flaming, baleful eyes riveted upon the black.

Mugambi, on his part, clung closely to Tarzan, so that the ape-man could scarce control his laughter at the pitiable condition to which the chief's fear had reduced him; but at length the white took the great cat by the scruff of the neck and, dragging it quite close to the Wagambi, slapped it sharply upon the nose each time that it growled at the stranger.

At the sight of the thing—a man mauling with his bare hands one of the most relentless and fierce of the jungle carnivora—Mugambi's eyes bulged from their sockets, and from entertaining a sullen respect for the giant white man who had made him prisoner, the black felt an almost worshipping awe of Tarzan.

The education of Sheeta progressed so well that in a short time Mugambi ceased to be the object of his hungry attention, and the black felt a degree more of safety in his society.

To say that Mugambi was entirely happy or at ease in his new environment would not be to adhere strictly to the truth. His eyes were constantly rolling apprehensively from side to side as now one and now another of the fierce pack chanced to wander near him, so that for the most of the time it was principally the whites that showed.

Together Tarzan and Mugambi, with Sheeta and Akut, lay in wait at the ford for a deer, and when at a word from the ape-man the four of them leaped out upon the affrighted animal the black was sure that the poor creature died of fright before ever one of the great beasts touched it.

Mugambi built a fire and cooked his portion of the kill; but Tarzan, Sheeta, and Akut tore theirs, raw, with their sharp teeth, growling among themselves when one ventured to encroach upon the share of another.

It was not, after all, strange that the white man's ways should have been so much more nearly related to those of the beasts than were the savage blacks. We are, all of us, creatures of habit, and when the seeming necessity for schooling ourselves in new ways ceases to exist, we fall naturally and easily into the manners and customs which long usage has implanted ineradicably within us.

Mugambi from childhood had eaten no meat until it had been cooked, while Tarzan, on the other hand, had never tasted cooked food of any sort until he had grown almost to manhood, and only within the past three or four years had he eaten cooked meat. Not only did the habit of a lifetime prompt him to eat it raw, but the craving of his palate as well; for to him cooked flesh was spoiled flesh when compared with the rich and juicy meat of a fresh, hot kill.

That he could, with relish, eat raw meat that had been buried by himself weeks before, and enjoy small rodents and disgusting grubs, seems to us who have been always "civilized" a revolting fact; but had we learned in childhood to eat these things, and had we seen all those about us eat them, they would seem no more sickening to us now than do many of our greatest dainties, at which a savage African cannibal would look with repugnance and turn up his nose.

For instance, there is a tribe in the vicinity of Lake Rudolph that will eat no sheep or cattle, though its next neighbours do so. Near by is another tribe that eats donkey-meat—a custom most revolting to the surrounding tribes that do not eat donkey. So who may say that it is nice to eat snails and frogs' legs and oysters, but disgusting to feed upon grubs and beetles, or that a raw oyster, hoof, horns, and tail, is less revolting than the sweet, clean meat of a fresh-killed buck?

The next few days Tarzan devoted to the weaving of a barkcloth sail with which to equip the canoe, for he despaired of being able to teach the apes to wield the paddles, though he did manage to get several of them to embark in the frail craft which he and Mugambi paddled about inside the reef where the water was quite smooth.

During these trips he had placed paddles in their hands, when they attempted to imitate the movements of him and Mugambi, but so difficult is it for them long to concentrate upon a thing that he soon saw that it would require weeks of patient training before they would be able to make any effective use of these new implements, if, in fact, they should ever do so.

There was one exception, however, and he was Akut. Almost from the first he showed an interest in this new sport that revealed a much higher plane of intelligence than that attained by any of his tribe. He seemed to grasp the purpose of the paddles, and when Tarzan saw that this was so he took much pains to explain in the meagre language of the anthropoid how they might be used to the best advantage.

From Mugambi Tarzan learned that the mainland lay but a short distance from the island. It seemed that the Wagambi warriors had ventured too far out in their frail craft, and when caught by a heavy tide and a high wind from offshore they had been driven out of sight of land. After paddling for a whole night, thinking that they were headed for home, they had seen this land at sunrise, and, still taking it for the mainland, had hailed it with joy, nor had Mugambi been aware that it was an island until Tarzan had told him that this was the fact.

The Wagambi chief was quite dubious as to the sail, for he had never seen such a contrivance used. His country lay far up the broad Ugambi River, and this was the first occasion that any of his people had found their way to the ocean.

Tarzan, however, was confident that with a good west wind he could navigate the little craft to the mainland. At any rate, he decided, it would be preferable to perish on the way than to remain indefinitely upon this evidently uncharted island to which no ships might ever be expected to come.

And so it was that when the first fair wind rose he embarked upon his cruise, and with him he took as strange and fearsome a crew as ever sailed under a savage master.

Mugambi and Akut went with him, and Sheeta, the panther, and a dozen great males of the tribe of Akut.

6

A Hideous Crew

THE war-canoe with its savage load moved slowly toward the break in the reef through which it must pass to gain the open sea. Tarzan, Mugambi, and Akut wielded the paddles, for the shore kept the west wind from the little sail.

Sheeta crouched in the bow at the ape-man's feet, for it had seemed best to Tarzan always to keep the wicked beast as far from the other members of the party as possible, since it would require little or no provocation to send him at the throat of any than the white man, whom he evidently now looked upon as his master.

In the stern was Mugambi, and just in front of him squatted Akut, while between Akut and Tarzan the twelve hairy apes sat upon their haunches, blinking dubiously this way and that, and now and then turning their eyes longingly back toward shore.

All went well until the canoe had passed beyond the reef. Here the breeze struck the sail, sending the rude craft lunging among the waves that ran higher and higher as they drew away from the shore.

With the tossing of the boat the apes became panic-stricken. They first moved uneasily about, and then commenced grumbling and whining. With difficulty Akut kept them in hand for a time; but when a particularly large wave struck the dugout simultaneoulsy with a little squall of wind their terror broke all bounds, and, leaping to their feet, they all but overturned the boat before Akut and Tarzan together could quiet them. At last calm was restored, and eventually the apes became accustomed to the strange antics of their craft, after which no more trouble was experienced with them.

The trip was uneventful, the wind held, and after ten hours' steady sailing the black shadows of the coast loomed close before the straining eyes of the ape-man in the bow. It was far too dark to distinguish whether they had approached close to the mouth of the Ugambi or not, so Tarzan ran in through the surf at the closest point to await the dawn.

The dugout turned broadside the instant that its nose touched the sand, and immediately it rolled over, with all its crew scrambling madly for the shore. The next breaker rolled them over and over, but eventually they all succeeded in crawling to safety, and in a moment more their ungainly craft had been washed up beside them.

The balance of the night the apes sat huddled close to one another for warmth; while Mugambi built a fire close to them over which he crouched. Tarzan and Sheeta, however, were of a different mind, for neither of them feared the jungle night, and the insistent craving of their hunger sent them off into the Stygian blackness of the forest in search of prey.

Side by side they walked where there was room for two abreast. At other times in single file, first one and then the other in advance. It was Tarzan who first caught the scent of meat—a bull buffalo—and presently the two came stealthily upon the sleeping beast in the midst of a dense jungle of reeds close to a river.

Closer and closer they crept toward the unsuspecting beast, Sheeta upon his right side and Tarzan upon his left nearest the great heart. They had hunted together now for some time, so that they worked in unison, with only low, purring sounds as signals.

For a moment they lay quite silent near their prey, and then at a sign from the ape-man Sheeta sprang upon the great back, burying his strong teeth in the bull's neck. Instantly the brute sprang to his feet with a bellow of pain and rage, and at the same instant Tarzan rushed in upon his left side with the stone knife, striking repeatedly behind the shoulder.

One of the ape-man's hands clutched the thick mane, and as the bull raced madly through the reeds the thing striking at his life was dragged beside him. Sheeta but clung tenaciously to his hold upon the neck and back, biting deep in an effort to reach the spine.

For several hundred yards the bellowing bull carried his two savage antagonists, until at last the blade found his heart, when with a final bellow that was half-scream he plunged headlong to the earth. Then Tarzan and Sheeta feasted to repletion.

After the meal the two curled up together in a thicket, the man's black head pillowed upon the tawny side of the panther. Shortly after dawn they awoke and ate again, and then returned to the beach that Tarzan might lead the balance of the pack to the kill.

When the meal was done the brutes were for curling up to sleep, so Tarzan and Mugambi set off in search of the Ugambi River. They had proceeded scarce a hundred yards when they came suddenly upon a broad stream, which the Negro instantly recognized as that down which he and his warriors had paddled to the sea upon their ill-starred expedition.

The two now followed the stream down to the ocean, finding that it emptied into a bay not over a mile from the point upon the beach at which the canoe had been thrown the night before.

Tarzan was much elated by the discovery, as he knew that in the vicinity of a large watercourse he should find natives, and from some of these he had little doubt but that he should obtain news of Rokoff and the child, for he felt reasonably certain that the Russian would rid himself of the baby as quickly as possible after having disposed of Tarzan.

He and Mugambi now righted and launched the dugout, though it was a most difficult feat in the face of the surf which rolled continuously in upon the beach; but at last they were successful, and soon after were paddling up the coast toward the mouth of the Ugambi. Here they experienced considerable difficulty in making an entrance against the combined current and ebb tide, but by taking advantage of eddies close in to shore they came about dusk to a point nearly opposite the spot where they had left the pack asleep.

Making the craft fast to an overhanging bough, the two made their way into the jungle, presently coming upon some of the apes feeding upon fruit a little beyond the reeds where the buffalo had fallen. Sheeta was not anywhere to be seen, nor did he return that night, so that Tarzan came to believe that he had wandered away in search of his own kind.

Early the next morning the ape-man led his band down to the river, and as he walked he gave vent to a series of shrill cries. Presently from a great distance and faintly there came an answering scream, and a half-hour later the lithe form of Sheeta bounded into view where the others of the pack were clambering gingerly into the canoe.

The great beast, with arched back and purring like a contented tabby, rubbed his sides against the ape-man, and then at a word from the latter sprang lightly to his former place in the bow of the dugout.

When all were in place it was discovered that two of the apes of Akut were missing, and though both the king ape and Tarzan called to them for the better part of an hour, there was no response, and finally the boat put off without them. As it happened that the two missing ones were the very same who had evinced the least desire to accompany the expedition from the island, and had suffered the most from fright during the voyage, Tarzan was quite sure that they had absented themselves purposely rather than again enter the canoe.

As the party were putting in for the shore shortly after noon to search for food a slender, naked savage watched them for a moment from behind the dense screen of verdure which lined the river's bank, then he melted away up-stream before any of those in the canoe discovered him.

Like a deer he bounded along the narrow trail until, filled with the excitement of his news, he burst into a native village several miles above the point at which Tarzan and his pack had stopped to hunt.

"Another white man is coming!" he cried to the chief who squatted before the entrance to his circular hut. "Another white man, and with him are many warriors. They come in a great war-canoe to kill and rob as did the black-bearded one who has just left us."

Kaviri leaped to his feet. He had but recently had a taste

of the white man's medicine, and his savage heart was filled with bitterness and hate. In another moment the rumble of the war-drums rose from the village, calling in the hunters from the forest and the tillers from the fields.

Seven war-canoes were launched and manned by paint-daubed, befeathered warriors. Long spears bristled from the rude battle-ships, as they slid noiselessly over the bosom of the water, propelled by giant muscles rolling beneath glistening, ebony hides.

There was no beating of tom-toms now, nor blare of native horn, for Kaviri was a crafty warrior, and it was in his mind to take no chances, if they could be avoided. He would swoop noiselessly down with his seven canoes upon the single one of the white man, and before the guns of the latter could inflict much damage upon his people he would have overwhelmed the enemy by force of numbers.

Kaviri's own canoe went in advance of the others a short distance, and as it rounded a sharp bend in the river where the swift current bore it rapidly on its way it came suddenly upon the thing that Kaviri sought.

So close were the two canoes to one another that the black had only an opportunity to note the white face in the bow of the oncoming craft before the two touched and his own men were upon their feet, yelling like mad devils and thrusting their long spears at the occupants of the other canoe.

But a moment later, when Kaviri was able to realize the nature of the crew that manned the white man's dugout, he would have given all the beads and iron wire that he possessed to have been safely within his distant village. Scarcely had the two craft come together than the frightful apes of Akut rose, growling and barking, from the bottom of the canoe, and, with long, hairy arms far outstretched, grasped the menacing spears from the hands of Kaviri's warriors.

The blacks were overcome with terror, but there was nothing to do other than to fight. Now came the other war-canoes rapidly down upon the two craft. Their occupants were eager to join the battle, for they thought that their foes were white men and their native porters.

They swarmed about Tarzan's craft; but when they saw the nature of the enemy all but one turned and paddled swiftly upriver. That one came too close to the ape-man's craft before its occupants realized that their fellows were pitted against demons instead of men. As it touched Tarzan spoke a few low words to Sheeta and Akut, so that before the attacking warriors could draw away there sprang upon them with a blood-freezing scream a huge panther, and into the other end of their canoe clambered a great ape.

At one end the panther wrought fearful havoc with his mighty talons and long, sharp fangs, while Akut at the other buried his yellow canines in the necks of those that came within his reach, hurling the terror-stricken blacks overboard as he made his way toward the centre of the canoe.

Kaviri was so busily engaged with the demons that had entered his own craft that he could offer no assistance to his warriors in the other. A giant of a white devil had wrested his spear from him as though he, the mighty Kaviri, had been but a new-born babe. Hairy monsters were overcoming his fighting men, and a black chieftain like himself was fighting shoulder to shoulder with the hideous pack that opposed him.

Kaviri battled bravely against his antagonist, for he felt that death had already claimed him, and so the least that he could do would be to sell his life as dearly as possible; but it was soon evident that his best was quite futile when pitted against the superhuman brawn and agility of the creature that at last found his throat and bent him back into the bottom of the canoe.

Presently Kaviri's head began to whirl—objects became confused and dim before his eyes—there was a great pain in his chest as he struggled for the breath of life that the thing upon him was shutting off for ever. Then he lost consciousness.

When he opened his eyes once more he found, much to his surprise, that he was not dead. He lay, securely bound, in the bottom of his own canoe. A great panther sat upon its haunches, looking down upon him.

Kaviri shuddered and closed his eyes again, waiting for the ferocious creature to spring upon him and put him out of his misery of terror.

After a moment, no rending fangs having buried themselves in his trembling body, he again ventured to open his eyes. Beyond the panther kneeled the white giant who had overcome him.

The man was wielding a paddle, while directly behind him Kaviri saw some of his own warriors similarly engaged. Back of them again squatted several of the hairy apes.

Tarzan, seeing that the chief had regained consciousness, addressed him.

"Your warriors tell me that you are the chief of a numerous people, and that your name is Kaviri," he said.

"Yes," replied the black.

"Why did you attack me? I came in peace."

"Another white man 'came in peace' three moons ago," replied Kaviri; "and after we had brought him presents of a goat and cassava and milk, he set upon us with his guns and killed many of my people, and then went on his way, taking all of our goats and many of our young men and women."

"I am not as this other white man," replied Tarzan. "I should not have harmed you had you not set upon me. Tell me, what was the face of this bad white man like? I am searching for one who has wronged me. Possibly this may be the very one."

"He was a man with a bad face, covered with a great, black beard, and he was very, very wicked—yes, very wicked indeed."

"Was there a little white child with him?" asked Tarzan, his heart almost stopping as he awaited the black's answer.

"No, *bwana*," replied Kaviri, "the white child was not with this man's party—it was with the other party."

"Other party!" exclaimed Tarzan. "What other party?"

"With the party that the very bad white man was pursuing. There was a white man, woman, and the child, with six Mosula porters. They passed up the river three days ahead of the very bad white man. I think that they were running away from him."

A white man, woman, and child! Tarzan was puzzled. The child must be his little Jack; but who could the woman be—and the man? Was it possible that one of Rokoff's confederates had conspired with some woman—who had accompanied the Russian—to steal the baby from him?

If this was the case, they had doubtless purposed returning the child to civilization and there either claiming a reward or holding the little prisoner for ransom.

But now that Rokoff had succeeded in chasing them far inland, up the savage river, there could be little doubt but that he would eventually overhaul them, unless, as was still more probable, they should be captured and killed by the very cannibals farther up the Ugambi, to whom, Tarzan was now convinced, it had been Rokoff's intention to deliver the baby.

As he talked to Kaviri the canoes had been moving steadily up-river toward the chief's village. Kaviri's warriors plied the paddles in the three canoes, casting sidelong, terrified glances at their hideous passengers. Three of the apes of Akut had been killed in the encounter, but there were, with Akut, eight of the frightful beasts remaining, and there was Sheeta, the panther, and Tarzan and Mugambi.

Kaviri's warriors thought that they had never seen so terrible a crew in all their lives. Momentarily they expected to be pounced upon and torn asunder by some of their captors; and, in fact, it was all that Tarzan and Mugambi and Akut could do to keep the snarling, ill-natured brutes from snapping at the glistening, naked bodies that brushed against them now and then with the movements of the paddlers, whose very fear added incitement to the beasts.

At Kaviri's camp Tarzan paused only long enough to eat the food that the blacks furnished, and arrange with the chief for a dozen men to man the paddles of his canoe.

Kaviri was only too glad to comply with any demands that the ape-man might make if only such compliance would hasten the departure of the horrid pack; but it was easier, he discovered, to promise men than to furnish them, for when his people learned his intentions those that had not already fled into the jungle proceeded to do so without loss of time, so that when Kaviri turned to point out those who were to accompany Tarzan, he discovered that he was the only member of his tribe left within the village.

Tarzan could not repress a smile.

"They do not seem anxious to accompany us," he said; "but just remain quietly here, Kaviri, and presently you shall see your people flocking to your side."

Then the ape-man rose, and, calling his pack about him, commanded that Mugambi remain with Kaviri, and disappeared in the jungle with Sheeta and the apes at his heels.

For half an hour the silence of the grim forest was broken only by the ordinary sounds of the teeming life that but adds to its lowering loneliness. Kaviri and Mugambi sat alone in the palisaded village, waiting.

Presently from a great distance came a hideous sound. Magumbi recognized the weird challenge of the ape-man. Immediately from different points of the compass rose a horrid semicircle of similar shrieks and screams, punctuated now and again by the blood-curdling cry of a hungry panther.

7

Betrayed

THE two savages, Kaviri and Mugambi, squatting before the entrance to Kaviri's hut, looked at one another—Kaviri with ill-concealed alarm.

"What is it?" he whispered.

"It is Bwana Tarzan and his people," replied Mugambi. "But what they are doing I know not, unless it be that they are devouring your people who ran away."

Kaviri shuddered and rolled his eyes fearfully toward the jungle. In all his long life in the savage forest he had never heard such an awful, fearsome din.

Closer and closer came the sounds, and now with them were mingled the terrified shrieks of women and children and of men. For twenty long minutes the blood-curdling cries continued, until they seemed but a stone's throw from the palisade. Kaviri rose to flee, but Mugambi seized and held him, for such had been the command of Tarzan.

A moment later a horde of terrified natives burst from the jungle, racing toward the shelter of their huts. Like frightened sheep they ran, and behind them, driving them as sheep might be driven, came Tarzan and Sheeta and the hideous apes of Akut.

Presently Tarzan stood before Kaviri, the old, quiet smile upon his lips.

"Your people have returned, my brother," he said, "and now you may select those who are to accompany me and paddle my canoe."

Tremblingly Kaviri tottered to his feet, calling to his people to come from their huts; but none responded to his summons.

"Tell them," suggested Tarzan, "that if they do not come I shall send my people in after them."

Kaviri did as he was bid, and in an instant the entire population of the village came forth, their wide and frightened eyes rolling from one to another of the savage creatures that wandered about the village street.

Quickly Kaviri designated a dozen warriors to accompany Tarzan. The poor fellows went almost white with terror at the prospect of close contact with the panther and the apes in the narrow confines of the canoes; but when Kaviri explained to them that there was no escape—that Bwana Tarzan would pursue them with his grim horde should they attempt to run away from the duty—they finally went gloomily down to the river and took their places in the canoe.

It was with a sigh of relief that their chieftain saw the party disappear about a headland a short distance up-river.

For three days the strange company continued farther and farther into the heart of the savage country that lies on either side of the almost unexplored Ugambi. Three of the twelve warriors deserted during that time; but as several of the apes had finally learned the secret of the paddles, Tarzan felt no dismay because of the loss.

As a matter of fact, he could have travelled much more rapidly on shore, but he believed that he could hold his own wild crew together to better advantage by keeping them to the boat as much as possible. Twice a day they landed to hunt and feed, and at night they slept upon the bank of the mainland or on one of the numerous little islands that dotted the river.

Before them the natives fled in alarm, so that they found only deserted villages in their path as they proceeded. Tarzan was anxious to get in touch with some of the savages who dwelt upon the river's banks, but so far he had been unable to do so.

Finally he decided to take to the land himself, leaving his company to follow after him by boat. He explained to Mugambi the thing that he had in mind, and told Akut to follow the directions of the black.

"I will join you again in a few days," he said. "Now I go ahead to learn what has become of the very bad white man whom I seek."

At the next halt Tarzan took to the shore, and was soon lost to the view of his people.

The first few villages he came to were deserted, showing that news of the coming of his pack had travelled rapidly; but toward evening he came upon a distant cluster of thatched huts surrounded by a rude palisade, within which were a couple of hundred natives.

The women were preparing the evening meal as Tarzan of the Apes poised above them in the branches of a giant tree which overhung the palisade at one point.

The ape-man was at a loss as to how he might enter into communication with these people without either frightening them or arousing their savage love of battle. He had no desire to fight now, for he was upon a much more important mission than that of battling with every chance tribe that he should happen to meet with.

At last he hit upon a plan, and after seeing that he was concealed from the view of those below, he gave a few hoarse grunts in imitation of a panther. All eyes immediately turned upward toward the foliage above.

It was growing dark, and they could not penetrate the leafy screen which shielded the ape-man from their view. The moment that he had won their attention he raised his voice in the shriller and more hideous scream of the beast he personated, and then, scarce stirring a leaf in his descent, dropped to the ground once again outside the palisade, and, with the speed of a deer, ran quickly round to the village gate.

Here he beat upon the fibre-bound saplings of which the barrier was constructed, shouting to the natives in their own tongue that he was a friend who wished food and shelter for the night.

Tarzan knew well the nature of the black man. He was aware that the grunting and screaming of Sheeta in the tree above them would set their nerves on edge, and that his pounding upon their gate after dark would still further add to their terror.

That they did not reply to his hail was no surprise, for natives are fearful of any voice that comes out of the night from beyond their palisades, attributing it always to some demon or other ghostly visitor; but still he continued to call.

"Let me in, my friends!" he cried. "I am a white man pursuing the very bad white man who passed this way a few days ago. I follow to punish him for the sins he has committed against you and me.

"If you doubt my friendship, I will prove it to you by going into the tree above your village and driving Sheeta back into the jungle before he leaps among you. If you will not promise to take me in and treat me as a friend I shall let Sheeta stay and devour you."

For a moment there was silence. Then the voice of an old man came out of the quiet of the village street.

"If you are indeed a white man and a friend, we will let you come in; but first you must drive Sheeta away."

"Very well," replied Tarzan. "Listen, and you shall hear Sheeta fleeing before me."

The ape-man returned quickly to the tree, and this time he made a great noise as he entered the branches, at the same time growling ominously after the manner of the panther, so that those below would believe that the great beast was still there.

When he reached a point well above the village street he made a great commotion, shaking the tree violently, crying aloud to the panther to flee or be killed, and punctuating his own voice with the screams and mouthings of an angry beast.

Presently he raced toward the opposite side of the tree and off into the jungle, pounding loudly against the boles of trees as he went, and voicing the panther's diminishing growls as he drew farther and farther away from the village.

A few minutes later he returned to the village gate, calling to the natives within.

"I have driven Sheeta away," he said. "Now come and admit me as you promised."

For a time there was the sound of excited discussion within the palisade, but at length a half-dozen warriors came and opened the gates, peering anxiously out in evident trepidation as to the nature of the creature which they should find waiting there. They were not much relieved at sight of an almost naked white man; but when Tarzan had reassured them in quiet tones, protesting his friendship for them, they opened the barrier a trifle farther and admitted him.

When the gates had been once more secured the self-confidence of the savages returned, and as Tarzan walked up the village street toward the chief's hut he was surrounded by a host of curious men, women, and children.

From the chief he learned that Rokoff had passed up the river a week previous, and that he had horns growing from his forehead, and was accompanied by a thousand devils. Later the chief said that the very bad white man had remained a month in his village.

Though none of these statements agreed with Kaviri's, that the Russian was but three days gone from the chieftain's village and that his following was much smaller than now stated, Tarzan was in no manner surprised at the discrepancies, for he was quite familiar with the savage mind's strange manner of functioning.

What he was most interested in knowing was that he was upon the right trail, and that it led toward the interior. In this circumstance he knew that Rokoff could never escape him.

After several hours of questioning and cross-questioning the ape-man learned that another party had preceded the Russian by several days—three whites—a man, a woman, and a little man-child, with several Mosulas.

Tarzan explained to the chief that his people would follow him in a canoe, probably the next day, and that though he might go on ahead of them the chief was to receive them kindly and have no fear of them, for Mugambi would see that they did not harm the chief's people, if they were accorded a friendly reception.

"And now," he concluded, "I shall lie down beneath this tree and sleep. I am very tired. Permit no one to disturb me."

The chief offered him a hut, but Tarzan, from past experience of native dwellings, preferred the open air, and, further, he had plans of his own that could be better carried out if he remained beneath the tree. He gave as his reason a desire to be close at hand should Sheeta return, and after this explanation the chief was very glad to permit him to sleep beneath the tree.

Tarzan had always found that it stood him in good stead to leave with natives the impression that he was to some extent possessed of more or less miraculous powers. He might easily have entered their village without recourse to the gates, but he believed that a sudden and unaccountable disappearance when he was ready to leave them would result in a more lasting impression upon their childlike minds, and so as soon as the village was quiet in sleep he rose, and, leaping into the branches of the tree above him, faded silently into the black mystery of the jungle night.

All the balance of that night the ape-man swung rapidly through the upper and middle terraces of the forest. When the going was good there he preferred the upper branches of the giant trees, for then his way was better lighted by the moon; but so accustomed were all his senses to the grim world of his birth that it was possible for him, even in the dense, black shadows near the ground, to move with ease and rapidity. You or I walking beneath the arcs of Main Street, or Broadway, or State Street, could not have moved more surely or with a tenth the speed of the agile ape-man through the gloomy mazes that would have baffled us entirely.

At dawn he stopped to feed, and then he slept for several hours, taking up the pursuit again toward noon.

Twice he came upon natives, and, though he had considerable difficulty in approaching them, he succeeded in each instance in quieting both their fears and bellicose intentions toward him, and learned from them that he was upon the trail of the Russian.

Two days later, still following up the Ugambi, he came upon a large village. The chief, a wicked-looking fellow with the sharp-filed teeth that often denote the cannibal, received him with apparent friendliness.

The ape-man was now thoroughly fatigued, and had determined to rest for eight or ten hours that he might be fresh and strong when he caught up with Rokoff, as he was sure he must do within a very short time.

The chief told him that the bearded white man had left his village only the morning before, and that doubtless he would be able to overtake him in a short time. The other party the chief had not seen or heard of, so he said.

Tarzan did not like the appearance or manner of the fellow, who seemed, though friendly enough, to harbour a certain contempt for this half-naked white man who came with no followers and offered no presents; but he needed the rest and food that the village would afford him with less effort than the jungle, and so, as he knew no fear of man, beast, or devil, he curled himself up in the shadow of a hut and was soon asleep.

Scarcely had he left the chief than the latter called two of his warriors, to whom he whispered a few instructions. A moment later the sleek, black bodies were racing along the river path, up-stream, toward the east.

In the village the chief maintained perfect quiet. He would permit no one to approach the sleeping visitor, nor any singing, nor loud talking. He was remarkably solicitous lest his guest be disturbed.

Three hours later several canoes came silently into view from up the Ugambi. They were being pushed ahead rapidly by the brawny muscles of their black crews. Upon the bank before the river stood the chief, his spear raised in a horizontal position above his head, as though in some manner of predetermined signal to those within the boats.

And such indeed was the purpose of his attitude—which meant that the white stranger within his village still slept peacefully.

In the bows of two of the canoes were the runners that the chief had sent forth three hours earlier. It was evident that they had been dispatched to follow and bring back this party, and that the signal from the bank was one that had been determined upon before they left the village.

In a few moments the dugouts drew up to the verdure-clad bank. The native warriors filed out, and with them a half-dozen white men. Sullen, ugly-looking customers they were, and none more so than the evil-faced, black-bearded man who commanded them.

"Where is the white man your messengers report to be with you?" he asked of the chief.

"This way, *bwana*," replied the native. "Carefully have I kept silence in the village that he might be still asleep when you returned. I do not know that he is one who seeks you to do you harm, but he questioned me closely about your coming and your going, and his appearance is as that of the one you described, but whom you believed safe in the country which you called Jungle Island.

"Had you not told me this tale I should not have recognized him, and then he might have gone after and slain you. If he is a friend and no enemy, then no harm has been done, *bwana*; but if he proves to be an enemy, I should like very much to have a rifle and some ammunition."

"You have done well," replied the white man, "and you shall have the rifle and ammunition whether he be a friend or enemy, provided that you stand with me."

"I shall stand with you, *bawana*," said the chief, "and now come and look upon the stranger, who sleeps within my village."

So saying, he turned and led the way toward the hut, in the shadow of which the unconscious Tarzan slept peacefully.

Behind the two men came the remaining whites and a score of warriors; but the raised forefingers of the chief and his companion held them all to perfect silence.

As they turned the corner of the hut, cautiously and upon tiptoe, an ugly smile touched the lips of the white as his eyes fell upon the giant figure of the sleeping ape-man.

The chief looked at the other inquiringly. The latter nodded his head, to signify that the chief had made no mistake in his suspicions. Then he turned to those behind him and, pointing to the sleeping man, motioned for them to seize and bind him.

A moment later a dozen brutes had leaped upon the surprised Tarzan, and so quickly did they work that he was securely bound before he could make half an effort to escape. Then they threw him down upon his back, and as his eyes turned toward the crowd that stood near, they fell upon the malign face of Nikolas Rokoff.

A sneer curled the Russian's lips. He stepped quite close to Trazan.

"Pig!" he cried. "Have you not yet learned sufficient wisdom to keep away from Nikolas Rokoff?"

Then he kicked the prostrate man full in the face.

"That for your welcome," he said.

"Tonight, before my Ethiop friends eat you, I shall tell you what has already befallen your wife and child, and what further plans I have for their futures."

8

The Dance of Death

THROUGH the luxuriant, tangled vegetation of the Stygian jungle night a great lithe body made its way sinuously and in utter silence upon its soft padded feet. Only two blazing points of yellow-green flame shone occasionally with the reflected light of the equatorial moon that now and again pierced the softly sighing roof rustling in the night wind.

Occasionally the beast would stop with high-held nose, sniffing searchingly. At other times a quick, brief incursion into the branches above delayed it momentarily in its steady journey toward the east. To its sensitive nostrils came the subtle unseen spoor of many a tender four-footed creature, bringing the slaver of hunger to the cruel, drooping jowl.

But steadfastly it kept on its way, strangely ignoring the cravings of appetite that at another time would have sent the rolling, fur-clad muscles flying at some soft throat.

All that night the creature pursued its lonely way, and the next day it halted only to make a single kill, which it tore to fragments and devoured with sullen, grumbling rumbles as though half famished for lack of food.

It was dusk when it approached the palisade that surrounded a large native village. Like the shadow of a swift and silent death it circled the village, nose to ground, halting at last close to the palisade, where it almost touched the backs of several huts. Here the beast sniffed for a moment, and then, turning its head upon one side, listened with up-pricked ears.

What it heard was no sound by the standards of human ears, yet to the highly attuned and delicate organs of the beast a message seemed to be borne to the savage brain. A won-drous transformation was wrought in the motionless mass of statuesque bone and muscle that had an instant before stood as though carved out of living bronze.

As if it had been poised upon steel springs, suddenly re-leased, it rose quickly and silently to the top of the palisade, disappearing, stealthily and catlike, into the dark space be-tween the wall and the back of an adjacent hut.

In the village street beyond women were preparing many little fires and fetching cooking-pots filled with water, for a great feast was to be celebrated ere the night was many hours older. About a stout stake near the centre of the circling fires a little knot of black warriors stood conversing, their bodies smeared with white and blue and ochre in broad and grotesque bands. Great circles of colour were drawn about their eyes and lips, their breasts and abdomens, and from their clay-plastered coiffures rose gay feathers and bits of long, straight wire.

The village was preparing for the feast, while in a hut at one side of the scene of the coming orgy the bound victim of their bestial appetites lay waiting for the end. And such an end!

Tarzan of the Apes, tensing his mighty muscles, strained at the bonds that pinioned him; but they had been re-en-forced many times at the instigation of the Russian, so that not even the ape-man's giant brawn could budge them.

Death!

Tarzan had looked the Hideous Hunter in the face many a time, and smiled. And he would smile again tonight when he knew the end was coming quickly; but now his thoughts were not of himself, but of those others—the dear ones who must suffer most because of his passing.

Jane would never know the manner of it. For that he thanked Heaven; and he was thankful also that she at least was safe in the heart of the world's greatest city. Safe among kind and loving friends who would do their best to lighten her misery.

But the boy!

Tarzan writhed at the thought of him. His son! And now he—the mighty Lord of the Jungle—he, Tarzan, King of the

Apes, the only one in all the world fitted to find and save the child from the horrors that Rokoff's evil mind had planned—had been trapped like a silly, dumb creature. He was to die in a few hours, and with him would go the child's last chance of succour.

Rokoff had been in to see and revile and abuse him several times during the afternoon; but he had been able to wring no word of remonstrance or murmur of pain from the lips of the giant captive.

So at last he had given up, reserving his particular bit of exquisite mental torture for the last moment, when, just before the savage spears of the cannibals should for ever make the object of his hatred immune to further suffering, the Russian planned to reveal to his enemy the true whereabouts of his wife whom he thought safe in England.

Dusk had fallen upon the village, and the ape-man could hear the preparations going forward for the torture and the feast. The dance of death he could picture in his mind's eye —for he had seen the thing many times in the past. Now he was to be the central figure, bound to the stake.

The torture of the slow death as the circling warriors cut him to bits with the fiendish skill, that mutilated without bringing unconsciousness, had no terrors for him. He was inured to suffering and to the sight of blood and to cruel death; but the desire to live was no less strong within him, and until the last spark of life should flicker and go out, his whole being would remain quick with hope and determination. Let them relax their watchfulness but for an instant, he knew that his cunning mind and giant muscles would find a way to escape—escape and revenge.

As he lay, thinking furiously on every possibility of self-salvation, there came to his sensitive nostrils a faint and a familiar scent. Instantly every faculty of his mind was upon the alert. Presently his trained ears caught the sound of the soundless presence without—behind the hut wherein he lay.

His lips moved, and though no sound came forth that might have been appreciable to a human ear beyond the walls of his prison, yet he realized that the one beyond would hear. Already he knew who that one was, for his nostrils had told him as plainly as your eyes or mine tell us of the identity of an old friend whom we come upon in broad daylight.

An instant later he heard the soft sound of a fur-clad body and padded feet scaling the outer wall behind the hut and then a tearing at the poles which formed the wall.

THE DANCE OF DEATH

Presently through the hole thus made slunk a great beast, pressing its cold muzzle close to his neck.

It was Sheeta, the panther.

The beast snuffed round the prostrate man, whining a little. There was a limit to the interchange of ideas which could take place between these two, and so Tarzan could not be sure that Sheeta understood all that he attempted to communicate to him. That the man was tied and helpless Sheeta could, of course, see; but that to the mind of the panther this would carry any suggestion of harm in so far as his master was concerned, Tarzan could not guess.

What had brought the beast to him? The fact that he had come augured well for what he might accomplish; but when Tarzan tried to get Sheeta to gnaw his bonds asunder the great animal could not seem to understand what was expected of him, and, instead, but licked the wrists and arms of the prisoner.

Presently there came an interruption. Some one was approaching the hut. Sheeta gave a low growl and slunk into the blackness of a far corner. Evidently the visitor did not hear the warning sound, for almost immediately he entered the hut—a tall, naked, savage warrior.

He came to Tarzan's side and pricked him with a spear. From the lips of the ape-man came a weird, uncanny sound, and in answer to it there leaped from the blackness of the hut's farthermost corner a bolt of fur-clad death. Full upon the breast of the painted savage the great beast struck, burying sharp talons in the black flesh and sinking great yellow fangs in the ebon throat.

There was a fearful scream of anguish and terror from the black, and mingled with it was the hideous challenge of the killing panther. Then came silence—silence except for the rending of bloody flesh and the crunching of human bones between mighty jaws.

The noise had brought sudden quiet to the village without. Then there came the sound of voices in consultation.

High-pitched, fear-filled voices, and deep, low tones of authority, as the chief spoke. Tarzan and the panther heard the approaching footsteps of many men, and then, to Tarzan's surprise, the great cat rose from across the body of its kill, and slunk noiselessly from the hut through the aperture through which it had entered.

The man heard the soft scraping of the body as it passed over the top of the palisade, and then silence. From the opposite side of the hut he heard the savages approaching to investigate.

He had little hope that Sheeta would return, for had the great cat intended to defend him against all comers it would have remained by his side as it heard the approaching savages without.

Tarzan knew how strange were the workings of the brains of the mighty carnivora of the jungle—how fiendishly fearless they might be in the face of certain death, and again how timid upon the slightest provocation. There was doubt in his mind that some note of the approaching blacks vibrating with fear had struck an answering chord in the nervous system of the panther, sending him slinking through the jungle, his tail between his legs.

The man shrugged. Well, what of it? He had expected to die, and, after all, what might Sheeta have done for him other than to maul a couple of his enemies before a rifle in the hands of one of the whites should have dispatched him!

If the cat could have released him! Ah! that would have resulted in a very different story; but it had proved beyond the understanding of Sheeta, and now the beast was gone and Tarzan must definitely abandon hope.

The natives were at the entrance to the hut now, peering fearfully into the dark interior. Two in advance held lighted torches in their left hands and ready spears in their right. They held back timorously against those behind, who were pushing them forward.

The shrieks of the panther's victim, mingled with those of the great cat, had wrought mightily upon their poor nerves, and now the awful silence of the dark interior seemed even more terribly ominous than had the frightful screaming.

Presently one of those who was being forced unwillingly within hit upon a happy scheme for learning first the precise nature of the danger which menaced him from the silent interior. With a quick movement he flung his lighted torch into the centre of the hut. Instantly all within was illuminated for a brief second before the burning brand was dashed out against the earth floor.

There was the figure of the white prisoner still securely bound as they had last seen him, and in the centre of the hut another figure equally as motionless, its throat and breasts horribly torn and mangled.

The sight that met the eyes of the foremost savages inspired more terror within their superstitious breasts than would the presence of Sheeta, for they saw only the result of a ferocious attack upon one of their fellows.

Not seeing the cause, their fear-ridden minds were free to attribute the ghastly work to supernatural causes, and with the thought they turned, screaming, from the hut, bowling over those who stood directly behind them in the exuberance of their terror.

For an hour Tarzan heard only the murmur of excited voices from the far end of the village. Evidently the savages were once more attempting to work up their flickering courage to a point that would permit them to make another invasion of the hut, for now and then came a savage yell, such as the warriors give to bolster up their bravery upon the field of battle.

But in the end it was two of the whites who first entered, carrying torches and guns. Tarzan was not surprised to discover that neither of them was Rokoff. He would have wagered his soul that no power on earth could have tempted that great coward to face the unknown menace of the hut.

When the natives saw that the white men were not attacked they, too, crowded into the interior, their voices hushed with terror as they looked upon the mutilated corpse of their comrade. The whites tried in vain to elicit an explanation from Tarzan; but to all their queries he but shook his head, a grim and knowing smile curving his lips.

At last Rokoff came.

His face grew very white as his eyes rested upon the bloody thing grinning up at him from the floor, the face set in a death mask of excruciating horror.

"Come!" he said to the chief. "Let us get to work and finish this demon before he has an opportunity to repeat this thing upon more of your people."

The chief gave orders that Tarzan should be lifted and carried to the stake; but it was several minutes before he could prevail upon any of his men to touch the prisoner.

At last, however, four of the younger warriors dragged Tarzan roughly from the hut, and once outside the pall of terror seemed lifted from the savage hearts.

A score of howling blacks pushed and buffeted the prisoner down the village street and bound him to the post in the centre of the circle of little fires and boiling cooking-pots.

When at last he was made fast and seemed quite helpless and beyond the faintest hope of succour, Rokoff's shrivelled wart of courage swelled to its usual proportions when danger was not present.

He stepped close to the ape-man, and, seizing a spear from the hands of one of the savages, was the first to prod the helpless victim. A little stream of blood trickled down the giant's smooth skin from the wound in his side; but no murmur of pain passed his lips.

The smile of contempt upon his face seemed to infuriate the Russian. With a volley of oaths he leaped at the helpless captive, beating him upon the face with his clenched fists and kicking him mercilessly about the legs.

Then he raised the heavy spear to drive it through the mighty heart, and still Tarzan of the Apes smiled contemptuously upon him.

Before Rokoff could drive the weapon home the chief sprang upon him and dragged him away from his intended victim.

"Stop, white man!" he cried. "Rob us of this prisoner and our death-dance, and you yourself may have to take his place."

The threat proved most effective in keeping the Russian from further assaults upon the prisoner, though he continued to stand a little apart and hurl taunts at his enemy. He told Tarzan that he himself was going to eat the ape-man's heart. He enlarged upon the horrors of the future life of Tarzan's son, and intimated that his vengeance would reach as well to Jane Clayton.

"You think your wife safe in England," said Rokoff. "Poor fool! She is even now in the hands of one not even of decent birth, and far from the safety of London and the protection of her friends. I had not meant to tell you this until I could bring to you upon Jungle Island proof of her fate.

"Now that you are about to die the most unthinkably horrid death that it is given a white man to die—let this word of the plight of your wife add to the torments that you must suffer before the last savage spear-thrust releases you from your torture."

The dance had commenced now, and the yells of the circling warriors drowned Rokoff's further attempts to distress his victim.

The leaping savages, the flickering firelight playing upon their painted bodies, circled about the victim at the stake.

To Tarzan's memory came a similar scene, when he had rescued D'Arnot from a like predicament at the last moment before the final spear-thrust should have ended his sufferings. Who was there now to rescue him? In all the world there was none able to save him from the torture and the death.

The thought that these human fiends would devour him when the dance was done caused him not a single qualm of horror or disgust. It did not add to his sufferings as it would have to those of an ordinary white man, for all his life

Tarzan had seen the beasts of the jungle devour the flesh of their kills.

Had he not himself battled for the grisly forearm of a great ape at that long-gone Dum-Dum, when he had slain the fierce Tublat and won his niche in the respect of the Apes of Kerchak?

The dancers were leaping more closely to him now. The spears were commencing to find his body in the first torturing pricks that prefaced the more serious thrusts.

It would not be long now. The ape-man longed for the last savage lunge that would end his misery.

And then, far out in the mazes of the weird jungle, rose a shrill scream.

For an instant the dancers paused, and in the silence of the interval there rose from the lips of the fast-bound white man an answering shriek, more fearsome and more terrible than that of the jungle-beast that had roused it.

For several minutes the blacks hesitated; then, at the urging of Rokoff and their chief, they leaped in to finish the dance and the victim; but ere ever another spear touched the brown hide a tawny streak of green-eyed hate and ferocity bounded from the door of the hut in which Tarzan had been imprisoned, and Sheeta, the panther, stood snarling beside his master.

For an instant the blacks and the whites stood transfixed with terror. Their eyes were riveted upon the bared fangs of the jungle cat.

Only Tarzan of the Apes saw what else there was emerging from the dark interior of the hut.

9

Chivalry or Villainy

FROM her cabin port upon the *Kincaid*, Jane Clayton had seen her husband rowed to the verdure-clad shore of Jungle Island, and then the ship once more proceeded upon its way.

For several days she saw no one other than Sven Anderssen, the *Kincaid's* taciturn and repellent cook. She asked him the name of the shore upon which her husband had been set.

"Ay tank it blow purty soon purty hard," replied the Swede, and that was all that she could get out of him.

She had come to the conclusion that he spoke no other English, and so she ceased to importune him for information; but never did she forget to greet him pleasantly or to thank him for the hideous, nauseating meals he brought her.

Three days from the spot where Tarzan had been marooned the *Kincaid* came to anchor in the mouth of a great river, and presently Rokoff came to Jane Clayton's cabin.

"We have arrived, my dear," he said, with a sickening leer. "I have come to offer you safety, liberty, and ease. My heart has been softened toward you in your suffering, and I would make amends as best I may.

"Your husband was a brute—you know that best who found him naked in his native jungle, roaming wild with the savage beasts that were his fellows. Now I am a gentleman, not only born of noble blood, but raised gently as befits a man of quality.

"To you, dear Jane, I offer the love of a cultured man and association with one of culture and refinement, which you must have sorely missed in your relations with the poor ape that through your girlish infatuation you married so thoughtlessly. I love you, Jane. You have but to say the word and no further sorrows shall afflict you—even your baby shall be returned to you unharmed."

Outside the door Sven Anderssen paused with the noonday meal he had been carrying to Lady Greystoke. Upon the end of his long, stringy neck his little head was cocked to one side, his close-set eyes were half closed, his ears, so expressive was his whole attitude of stealthy eavesdropping, seemed truly to be cocked forward—even his long, yellow, straggly moustache appeared to assume a sly droop.

As Rokoff closed his appeal, awaiting the reply he invited, the look of surprise upon Jane Clayton's face turned to one of disgust. She fairly shuddered in the fellow's face.

"I would not have been surprised, M. Rokoff," she said, "had you attempted to force me to submit to your evil desires, but that you should be so fatuous as to believe that I, wife of John Clayton, would come to you willingly, even to save my life, I should never have imagined. I have known you for a scoundrel, M. Rokoff; but until now I had not taken you for a fool."

Rokoff's eyes narrowed, and the red of mortification

flushed out the pallor of his face. He took a step toward the girl, threateningly.

"We shall see who is the fool at last," he hissed, "when I have broken you to my will and your plebeian Yankee stubbornness has cost you all that you hold dear—even the life of your baby—for, by the bones of St. Peter, I'll forego all that I had planned for the brat and cut its heart out before your very eyes. You'll learn what it means to insult Nikolas Rokoff."

Jane Clayton turned wearily away.

"What is the use," she said, "of expatiating upon the depths to which your vengeful nature can sink? You cannot move me either by threats or deeds. My baby cannot judge yet for himself, but I, his mother, can foresee that should it have been given him to survive to man's estate he would willingly sacrifice his life for the honour of his mother. Love him as I do, I would not purchase his life at such a price. Did I, he would execrate my memory to the day of his death."

Rokoff was now thoroughly angered because of his failure to reduce the girl to terror. He felt only hate for her, but it had come to his diseased mind that if he could force her to accede to his demands as the price of her life and her child's, the cup of his revenge would be filled to brimming when he could flaunt the wife of Lord Greystoke in the capitals of Europe as his mistress.

Again he stepped closer to her. His evil face was convulsed with rage and desire. Like a wild beast he sprang upon her, and with his strong fingers at her throat forced her backward upon the berth.

At the same instant the door of the cabin opened noisily. Rokoff leaped to his feet, and, turning, faced the Swede cook.

Into the fellow's usually foxy eyes had come an expression of utter stupidity. His lower jaw drooped in vacuous harmony. He busied himself in arranging Lady Greystoke's meal upon the tiny table at one side of her cabin.

The Russian glared at him.

"What do you mean," he cried, "by entering here without permission? Get out!"

The cook turned his watery blue eyes upon Rokoff and smiled vacuously.

"Ay tank it blow purty soon purty hard," he said, and then he began rearranging the few dishes upon the little table.

"Get out of here, or I'll throw you out, you miserable

blockhead!" roared Rokoff, taking a threatening step toward the Swede.

Anderssen continued to smile foolishly in his direction, but one harm-like paw slid stealthily to the handle of the long, slim knife that protruded from the greasy cord supporting his soiled apron.

Rokoff saw the move and stopped short in his advance. Then he turned toward Jane Clayton.

"I will give you until tomorrow," he said, "to reconsider your answer to my offer. All will be sent ashore upon one pretext or another except you and the child, Paulvitch and myself. Then without interruption you will be able to witness the death of the baby."

He spoke in French that the cook might not understand the sinister portent of his words. When he had done he banged out of the cabin without another look at the man who had interrupted him in his sorry work.

When he had gone, Sven Anderssen turned toward Lady Greystoke—the idiotic expression that had masked his thoughts had fallen away, and in its place was one of craft and cunning.

"Hay tank Ay ban a fool," he said. "Hay ban the fool. Ay savvy Franch."

Jane Clayton looked at him in surprise.

"You understood all that he said, then?"

Anderssen grinned.

"You bat," he said.

"And you heard what was going on in here and came to protect me?"

"You bane good to me," explained the Swede. "Hay treat me like darty dog. Ay help you, lady. You yust vait—Ay help you. Ay ban Vast Coast lots times."

"But how can you help me, Sven," she asked, "when all these men will be against us?"

"Ay tank," said Sven Anderssen, "it blow purty soon purty hard," and then he turned and left the cabin.

Though Jane Clayton doubted the cook's ability to be of any material service to her, she was nevertheless deeply grateful to him for what he already had done. The feeling that among these enemies she had one friend brought the first ray of comfort that had come to lighten the burden of her miserable apprehensions throughout the long voyage of the *Kincaid*.

She saw no more of Rokoff that day, nor of any other until Sven came with her evening meal. She tried to draw him into conversation relative to his plans to aid her, but all that she could get from his was his stereotyped prophecy as to the future state of the wind. He seemed suddenly to have relapsed into his wonted state of dense stupidity.

However, when he was leaving her cabin a little later with the empty dishes he whispered very low, "Leave on your clothes an' roll up your blankets. Ay come back after you purty soon."

He would have slipped from the room at once, but Jane laid her hand upon his sleeve.

"My baby?" she asked. "I cannot go without him."

"You do wot Ay tal you," said Anderssen, scowling. "Ay ban halpin' you, so don't you gat too fonny."

When he had gone Jane Clayton sank down upon her berth in utter bewilderment. What was she to do? Suspicions as to the intentions of the Swede swarmed her brain. Might she not be infinitely worse off if she gave herself into his power than she already was?

No, she could be no worse off in company with the devil himself than with Nikolas Rokoff, for the devil at least bore the reputation of being a gentleman.

She swore a dozen times that she would not leave the *Kincaid* without her baby, and yet she remained clothed long past her usual hour for retiring, and her blankets were neatly rolled and bound with stout cord, when about midnight there came a stealthy scratching upon the panels of her door.

Swiftly she crossed the room and drew the bolt. Softly the door swung open to admit the muffled figure of the Swede. On one arm he carried a bundle, evidently his blankets. His other hand was raised in a gesture commanding silence, a grimy forefinger upon his lips.

He came quite close to her.

"Carry this," he said. "Do not make some noise when you see it. It ban your kid."

Quick hands snatched the bundle from the cook, and hungry mother arms folded the sleeping infant to her breast, while hot tears of joy ran down her cheeks and her whole frame shook with the emotion of the moment.

"Come!" said Anderssen. "We got no time to vaste."

He snatched up her bundle of blankets, and outside the cabin door his own as well. Then he led her to the ship's side, steadied her descent of the monkey-ladder, holding the child for her as she climbed to the waiting boat below. A moment later he had cut the rope that held the small boat to the steamer's side, and, bending silently to the muffled oars, was pulling toward the black shadows up the Ugambi River.

Anderssen rowed on as though quite sure of his ground,

and when after half an hour the moon broke through the
clouds there was revealed upon their left the mouth of a
tributary running into the Ugambi. Up this narrow channel
the Swede turned the prow of the small boat.

Jane Clayton wondered if the man knew where he was
bound. She did not know that in his capacity as cook he had
that day been rowed up this very steam to a little village
where he had bartered with the natives for such provisions
as they had for sale, and that he had there arranged the details of his plan for the adventure upon which they were now
setting forth.

Even though the moon was full, the surface of the small
river was quite dark. The giant trees overhung its narrow
banks, meeting in a great arch above the centre of the river.
Spanish moss dropped from the gracefully bending limbs,
and enormous creepers clambered in riotous profusion from
the ground to the loftiest branch, falling in curving loops
almost to the water's placid breast.

Now and then the river's surface would be suddenly
broken ahead of them by a huge crocodile, startled by the
splashing of the oars, or, snorting and blowing, a family of
hippos would dive from a sandy bar to the cool, safe depths
of the bottom.

From the dense jungles upon either side came the weird
night cries of the carnivora—the maniacal voice of the
hyena, the coughing grunt of the panther, the deep and
awful roar of the lion. And with them strange, uncanny
notes that the girl could not ascribe to any particular night
prowler—more terible because of their mystery.

Huddled in the stern of the boat she sat with her baby
strained close to her bosom, and because of that little
tender, helpless thing she was happier tonight than she had
been for many a sorrow-ridden day.

Even though she knew not to what fate she was going, or
how soon that fate might overtake her, still was she happy
and thankful for the moment, however brief, that she might
press her baby tightly in her arms. She could scarce wait
for the coming of the day that she might look again upon the
bright face of her little, black-eyed Jack.

Again and again she tried to strain her eyes through the
blackness of the jungle night to have but a tiny peep at those
beloved features, but only the dim outline of the baby face
rewarded her efforts. Then once more she would cuddle the
warm, little bundle close to her throbbing heart.

It must have been close to three o'clock in the morning
that Anderssen brought the boat's nose to the shore before a

clearing where could be dimly seen in the waning moon-light a cluster of native huts encircled by a thorn *boma*.

The Swede called out a number of times before he could obtain a reply from the village, and then only because he had been expected, so fearful are the natives of voices out of the darkness of the night. He helped Jane Clayton ashore with the baby, tied the boat to a small bush, and, picking up their blankets, led her toward the *boma*.

At the village gate they were admitted by a native woman, the wife of the chief whom Anderssen had paid to assist him. She took them to the chief's hut, but Anderssen said that they would sleep without upon the ground, and so, her duty having been completed, she left them to their own de-vices.

The Swede, after explaining in his gruff way that the huts were doubtless filthy and vermin-ridden, spread Jane's blan-kets on the ground for her, and at a little distance unrolled his own and lay down to sleep.

It was some time before the girl could find a comfortable position upon the hard ground, but at last, the baby in the hollow of her arm, she dropped asleep from utter exhaustion.

When she awoke it was broad daylight.

About her were clustered a score of curious natives—mostly men, for among the aborigines it is the male who owns this characteristic in its most exaggerated form. In-stinctively Jane Clayton drew the baby more closely to her, though she soon saw that the blacks were far from intend-ing her or the child any harm.

In fact, one of them offered her a gourd of milk—a filthy, smoke-begrimed gourd, with the ancient rind of long-curdled milk caked in layers within its neck; but the spirit of the giver touched her deeply, and her face lightened for a mom-ent with one of those almost forgotten smiles of radiance that had helped to make her beauty famous both in Balti-more and London.

She took the gourd in one hand, and rather than cause the giver pain raised it to her lips, though for the life of her she could scarce restrain the qualm of nausea that surged through her as the malodorous thing approached her nostrils.

It was Anderssen who came to her rescue, and taking the gourd from her, drank a portion himself, and then returned it to the native with a gift of blue beads.

The sun was shining brightly now, and though the baby still slept, Jane could scarce restrain her impatient desire to have at least a brief glance at the beloved face. The natives had withdrawn at a command from their chief, who now stood talking with Anderssen, a little apart from her.

As she debated the wisdom of risking disturbing the child's slumber by lifting the blanket that now protected its face from the sun, she noted that the cook conversed with the chief in the language of the Negro.

What a remarkable man the fellow was, indeed! She had thought him ignorant and stupid but a short day before, and now, within the past twenty-four hours, she had learned that he spoke not only English but French as well, and the primitive dialect of the West Coast.

She had thought him shifty, cruel, and untrustworthy, yet in so far as she had reason to believe he had proved himself in every way the contrary since the day before. It scarce seemed credible that he could be serving her from motives purely chivalrous. There must be something deeper in his intentions and plans than he had yet disclosed.

She wondered, and when she looked at him—at his close-set, shifty eyes and repulsive features, she shuddered, for she was convinced that no lofty characteristics could be hid behind so foul an exterior.

As she was thinking of these things the while she debated the wisdom of uncovering the baby's face, there came a little grunt from the wee bundle in her lap, and then a gurgling coo that set her heart in raptures.

The baby was awake! Now she might feast her eyes upon him.

Quickly she snatched the blanket from before the infant's face; Anderssen was looking at her as she did so.

He saw her stagger to her feet, holding the baby at arm's length from her, her eyes glued in horror upon the little chubby face and twinkling eyes.

Then he heard her piteous cry as her knees gave beneath her, and she sank to the ground in a swoon.

10

The Swede

AS the warriors, clustered thick about Tarzan and Sheeta, realized that it was a flesh-and-blood panther that had interrupted their dance of death, they took heart a trifle, for in the face of all those circling spears even the mighty Sheeta would be doomed.

Rokoff was urging the chief to have his spearmen launch their missiles, and the black was upon the instant of issuing the command, when his eyes strayed beyond Tarzan, following the gaze of the ape-man.

With a yell of terror the chief turned and fled toward the village gate, and as his people looked to see the cause of his fright, they too took to their heels—for there, lumbering down upon them, their huge forms exaggerated by the play of moonlight and camp fire, came the hideous apes of Akut.

The instant the natives turned to flee the ape-man's savage cry rang out above the shrieks of the blacks, and in answer to it Sheeta and the apes leaped growling after the fugitives. Some of the warriors turned to battle with their enraged antagonists, but before the fiendish ferocity of the fierce beasts they went down to bloody death.

Others were dragged down in their flight, and it was not until the village was empty and the last of the blacks had disappeared into the bush that Tarzan was able to recall his savage pack to his side. Then it was that he discovered to his chagrin that he could not make one of them, not even the comparatively intelligent Akut, understand that he wished to be freed from the bonds that held him to the stake.

In time, of course, the idea would filter through their thick skulls, but in the meanwhile many things might happen—the blacks might return in force to regain their village; the whites might readily pick them all off with their rifles from the surrounding trees; he might even starve to death before the dull-witted apes realized that he wished them to gnaw through his bonds.

As for Sheeta—the great cat understood even less than the apes; but yet Tarzan could not but marvel at the remarkable characteristics this beast had evidenced. That it felt real affection for him there seemed little doubt, for now that the blacks were disposed of it walked slowly back and forth about the stake, rubbing its sides against the ape-man's legs and purring like a contented tabby. That it had gone of its own volition to bring the balance of the pack to his rescue, Tarzan could not doubt. His Sheeta was indeed a jewel among beasts.

Mugambi's absence worried the ape-man not a little. He attempted to learn from Akut what had become of the black, fearing that the beasts, freed from the restraint of Tarzan's presence, might have fallen upon the man and devoured him; but to all his questions the great ape but pointed back in the direction from which they had come out of the jungle.

The night passed with Tarzan still fast bound to the stake, and shortly after dawn his fears were realized in the discovery of naked black figures moving stealthily just within the edge of the jungle about the village. The blacks were returning.

With daylight their courage would be equal to the demands of a charge upon the handful of beasts that had routed them from their rightful abodes. The result of the encounter seemed foregone if the savages could curb their superstitious terror, for against their overwhelming numbers, their long spears and poisoned arrows, the panther and the apes could not be expected to survive a really determined attack.

That the black were preparing for a charge became apparent a few moments later, when they commenced to show themselves in force upon the edge of the clearing, dancing and jumping about as they waved their spears and shouted taunts and fierce warcries toward the village.

These manoeuvres Tarzan knew would continue until the blacks had worked themselves into a state of hysterical courage sufficient to sustain them for a short charge toward the village, and even though he doubted that they would reach it at the first attempt, he believed that at the second or the third they would swarm through the gateway, when the outcome could not be aught than the extermination of Tarzan's bold, but unarmed and undisciplined, defenders.

Even as he had guessed, the first charge carried the howling warriors but a short distance into the open—a shrill, weird challenge from the ape-man being all that was necessary to send them scurrying back to the bush. For half an hour they pranced and yelled their courage to the sticking-point, and again essayed a charge.

This time they came quite to the village gate, but when Sheeta and the hideous apes leaped among them they turned screaming in terror, and again fled to the jungle.

Again was the dancing and shouting repeated. This time Tarzan felt no doubt they would enter the village and complete the work that a handful of determined white men would have carried to a successful conclusion at the first attempt.

To have rescue come so close only to be thwarted because he could not make his poor, savage friends understand precisely what he wanted of them was most irritating, but he could not find it in his heart to place blame upon them. They had done their best, and now he was sure they would doubtless remain to die with him in a fruitless effort to defend him.

The blacks were already preparing for the charge. A few individuals had advanced a short distance toward the village and were exhorting the others to follow them. In a moment the whole savage horde would be racing across the clearing.

Tarzan thought only of the little child somewhere in this cruel, relentless wilderness. His heart ached for the son that he might no longer seek to save—that and the realization of Jane's suffering were all that weighed upon his brave spirit in these that he thought his last moments of life. Succour, all that he could hope for, had come to him in the instant of his extremity—and failed. There was nothing further for which to hope.

The blacks were half-way across the clearing when Tarzan's attention was attracted by the actions of one of the apes. The beast was glaring toward one of the huts. Tarzan followed his gaze. To his infinite relief and delight he saw the stalwart form of Mugambi racing toward him.

The huge black was panting heavily as though from strenuous physical exertion and nervous excitement. He rushed to Tarzan's side, and as the first of the savages reached the village gate the native's knife severed the last of the cords that bound Tarzan to the stake.

In the street lay the corpses of the savages that had fallen before the pack the night before. From one of these Tarzan seized a spear and knob stick, and with Mugambi at his side and the snarling pack about him, he met the natives as they poured through the gate.

Fierce and terrile was the battle that ensued, but at last the savages were routed, more by terror, perhaps, at sight of a black man and a white fighting in company with a panther and the huge fierce apes of Akut, than because of their inability to overcome the relatively small force that opposed them.

One prisoner fell into the hands of Tarzan, and him the ape-man questioned in an effort to learn what had become of Rokoff and his party. Promised his liberty in return for the information, the black told all he knew concerning the movements of the Russian.

It seemed that early in the morning their chief had attempted to prevail upon the whites to return with him to the village and with their guns destroy the ferocious pack that had taken possession of it, but Rokoff appeared to entertain even more fears of the giant white man and his strange companions than even the blacks themselves.

Upon no conditions would he consent to returning even within sight of the village. Instead, he took his party hurriedly to the river, where they stole a number of canoes the blacks had hidden there. The last that had been seen of them they had been paddling strongly up-stream, their porters from Kaviri's village wielding the blades.

So once more Tarzan of the Apes with his hideous pack took up his search for the ape-man's son and the pursuit of his abductor.

For weary days they followed through an almost uninhabited country, only to learn at last that they were upon the wrong trail. The little band had been reduced by three, for three of Akut's apes had fallen in the fighting at the village. Now, with Akut, there were five great apes, and Sheeta was there—and Mugambi and Tarzan.

The ape-man no longer heard rumours even of the three who had preceded Rokoff—the white man and woman and the child. Who the man and woman were he could not guess, but that the child was his was enough to keep him hot upon the trail. He was sure that Rokoff would be following this trio, and so he felt confident that so long as he could keep upon the Russian's trail he would be winning so much nearer to the time he might snatch his son from the dangers and horrors that menaced him.

In retracing their way after losing Rokoff's trail Tarzan picked it up again at a point where the Russian had left the river and taken to the brush in a northerly direction. He could only account for this change on the ground that the child had been carried away from the river by the two who now had possession of it.

Nowhere along the way, however, could he gain definite information that might assure him positively that the child was ahead of him. Not a single native they questioned had seen or heard of this other party, though nearly all had had direct experience with the Russian or had talked with others who had.

It was with difficulty that Tarzan could find means to communicate with the natives, as the moment their eyes fell upon his companions they fled precipitately into the bush. His only alternative was to go ahead of his pack and waylay an occasional warrior whom he found alone in the jungle.

One day as he was thus engaged, tracking an unsuspecting savage, he came upon the fellow in the act of hurling a spear at a wounded white man who crouched in a clump of bush at the trail's side. The white was one whom Tarzan had often seen, and whom he recognized at once.

Deep in his memory was implanted those repulsive features—the close-set eyes, the shifty expression, the drooping yellow moustache.

Instantly it occurred to the ape-man that this fellow had not been among those who had accompanied Rokoff at the village where Tarzan had been a prisoner. He had seen them all, and this fellow had not been there. There could be but one explanation—he it was who had fled ahead of the Russian with the woman and the child—and the woman had been Jane Clayton. He was sure now of the meaning of Rokoff's words.

The ape-man's face went white as he looked upon the pasty, vice-marked countenance of the Swede. Across Tarzan's forehead stood out the broad band of scarlet that marked the scar where, years before, Terkoz had torn a great strip of the ape-man's scalp from his skull in the fierce battle in which Tarzan had sustained his fitness to the kingship of the apes of Kerchak.

The man was his prey—the black should not have him, and with the thought he leaped upon the warrior, striking down the spear before it could reach its mark. The black, whipping out his knife, turned to do battle with this new enemy, while the Swede, lying in the bush, witnessed a duel, the like of which he had never dreamed to see—a half-naked white man battling with a half-naked black, hand to hand with the crude weapons of primeval man at first, and then with hands and teeth like the primordial brutes from whose loins their forebears sprung.

For a time Anderssen did not recognize the white, and when at last it dawned upon him that he had seen this giant before, his eyes went wide in surprise that this growling, rending beast could ever have been the well-groomed English gentleman who had been a prisoner aboard the *Kincaid*.

An English nobleman! He had learned the identity of the *Kincaid's* prisoners from Lady Greystoke during their flight up the Ugambi. Before, in common with the other members of the crew of the steamer, he had not known who the two might be.

The fight was over. Tarzan had been compelled to kill his antagonist, as the fellow would not surrender.

The Swede saw the white man leap to his feet beside the corpse of his foe, and placing one foot upon the broken neck lift his voice in the hideous challenge of the victorious bull-ape.

Anderssen shuddered. Then Tarzan turned toward him. His face was cold and cruel, and in the grey eyes the Swede read murder.

"Where is my wife?" growled the ape-man. "Where is the child?"

Anderssen tried to reply, but a sudden fit of coughing choked him. There was an arrow entirely through his chest, and as he coughed the blood from his wounded lung poured suddenly from his mouth and nostrils.

Tarzan stood waiting for the paroxysm to pass. Like a bronze image—cold, hard, and relentless—he stood over the helpless man, waiting to wring such information from him as he needed, and then to kill.

Presently the coughing and the haemorrhage ceased, and again the wounded man tried to speak. Tarzan knelt near the faintly moving lips.

"The wife and child!" he repeated. "Where are they?"

Anderssen pointed up the trail.

"The Russian—he got them," he whispered.

"How did you come here?" continued Tarzan. "Why are you not with Rokoff?"

"They catch us," replied Anderssen, in a voice so low that the ape-man could just distinguish the words. "They catch us. Ay fight, but my men they all run avay. Then they get me when Ay ban vounded. Rokoff he say leave me here for the hyenas. That vas vorse than to kill. He tak your vife and kid."

"What were you doing with them—where were you taking them?" asked Tarzan, and then, fiercely, leaping close to the fellow with fierce eyes blazing with the passion of hate and vengeance that he had with difficulty controlled, "What harm did you do to my wife or child? Speak quick before I kill you! Make your peace with God! Tell me the worst, or I will tear you to pieces with my hands and teeth. You have seen that I can do it!"

A look of wide-eyed surprise overspread Anderssen's face.

"Why," he whispered, "Ay did not hurt them. Ay tried to save them from that Russian. Your vife was kind to me on the *Kincaid,* and Ay hear that little baby cry sometimes. Ay got a vife an' kid for my own by Christiania an' Ay couldn't bear for to see them separated an' in Rokoff's hands any more. That vas all. Do Ay look like Ay ban here to hurt them?" he continued after a pause, pointing to the arrow protruding from his breast.

There was something in the man's tone and expression that convinced Tarzan of the truth of his assertions. More weighty than anything else was the fact that Anderssen evidently seemed more hurt than frightened. He knew he was going to die, so Tarzan's threats had little effect upon him; but it was quite apparent that he wished the Englishman to know the truth and not to wrong him by harbouring the belief that his words and manner indicated that he had entertained.

The ape-man instantly dropped to his knees beside the Swede.

"I am sorry," he said very simply. "I had looked for none but knaves in company with Rokoff. I see that I was wrong. That is past now, and we will drop it for the more important matter of getting you to a place of comfort and looking after your wounds. We must have you on your feet again as soon as possible."

The Swede, smiling, shook his head.

"You go on an' look for the vife an' kid," he said. "Ay ban as gude as dead already; but"—he hesitated—"Ay hate to think of the hyenas. Von't you finish up this job?"

Tarzan shuddered. A moment ago he had been upon the point of killing this man. Now he could no more have taken his life than he could have taken the life of any of his best friends.

He lifted the Swede's head in his arms to change and ease his position.

Again came a fit of coughing and the terrible haemorrhage. After it was over Anderssen lay with closed eyes.

Tarzan thought that he was dead, until he suddenly raised his eyes to those of the ape-man, sighed, and spoke—in a very low, weak whisper:

"Ay tank it blow purty soon purty hard!" he said, and died.

11

Tambudza

TARZAN scooped a shallow grave for the *Kincaid's* cook, beneath whose repulsive exterior had beaten the heart of a chivalrous gentleman. That was all he could do in the cruel jungle for the man who had given his life in the service of his little son and his wife.

Then Tarzan took up again the pursuit of Rokoff. Now that he was positive that the woman ahead of him was indeed Jane, and that she had again fallen into the hands of the Russian, it seemed that with all the incredible speed of his fleet and agile muscles he moved at but a snail's pace.

It was with difficulty that he kept the trail, for there were many paths through the jungle at this point—crossing and crisscrossing, forking and branching in all directions, and over them all had passed natives innumerable, coming and going. The spoor of the white men was obliterated by that of the native carriers who had followed them, and over all was the spoor of other natives and of wild beasts.

It was most perplexing; yet Tarzan kept on assiduously, checking his sense of sight against his sense of smell, that he might more surely keep to the right trail. But, with all his care, night found him at a point where he was positive that he was on the wrong trail entirely.

He knew that the pack would follow his spoor, and so he had been careful to make it as distinct as possible, brushing often against the vines and creepers that walled the jungle-path, and in other ways leaving his scent-spoor plainly discernible.

As darkness settled a heavy rain set in, and there was nothing for the baffled ape-man to do but wait in the partial shelter of a huge tree until morning; but the coming of dawn brought no cessation of the torrential downpour.

For a week the sun was obscured by heavy clouds, while violent rain and wind storms obliterated the last remnants of the spoor Tarzan constantly though vainly sought.

During all this time he saw no signs of natives, nor of his own pack, the members of which he feared had lost his trail during the terrific storm. As the country was strange to him, he had been unable to judge his course accurately, since he had had neither sun by day nor moon nor stars by night to guide him.

When the sun at last broke through the clouds in the forenoon of the seventh day, it looked down upon an almost frantic ape-man.

For the first time in his life, Tarzan of the Apes had been lost in the jungle. That the experience should have befallen him at such a time seemed cruel beyond expression. Somewhere in this savage land his wife and son lay in the clutches of the arch-fiend Rokoff.

What hideous trials might they not have undergone during those seven awful days that nature had thwarted him in his endeavours to locate them? Tarzan knew the Russian, in whose power they were, so well that he could not doubt but that the man, filled with rage that Jane had once escaped him, and knowing that Tarzan might be close upon his trail, would wreak without further loss of time whatever vengeance his polluted mind might be able to conceive.

But now that the sun shone once more, the ape-man was still at a loss as to what direction to take. He knew that Rokoff had left the river in pursuit of Anderssen, but whether he would continue inland or return to the Ugambi was a question.

The ape-man had seen that the river at the point he had left it was growing narrow and swift, so that he judged that it could not be navigable even for canoes to any great distance farther toward its source. However, if Rokoff had not returned to the river, in what direction had he proceeded?

From the direction of Anderssen's flight with Jane and the child Tarzan was convinced that the man had purposed attempting the tremendous feat of crossing the continent to Zanzibar; but whether Rokoff would dare so dangerous a journey or not was a question.

Fear might drive him to the attempt now that he knew the manner of horrible pack that was upon his trail, and that Tarzan of the Apes was following him to wreak upon him the vengeance that he deserved.

At last the ape-man determined to continue toward the northeast in the general direction of German East Africa until he came upon natives from whom he might gain information as to Rokoff's whereabouts.

The second day following the cessation of the rain came upon a native village the inhabitants of which fled into the bush the instant their eyes fell upon him. Tarzan, not to be thwarted in any such manner as this, pursued them, and after a brief chase caught up with a young warrior. The fellow was so badly frightened that he was unable to defend himself, dropping his weapons and falling upon the ground, wide-eyed and screaming as he gazed on his captor.

It was with considerable difficulty that the ape-man quieted the fellow's fears sufficiently to obtain a coherent statement from him as to the cause of his uncalled-for terror.

From him Tarzan learned, by dint of much coaxing, that a party of whites had passed through the village several days before. These men had told them of a terrible white devil that pursued them, warning the natives against it and the frightful pack of demons that accompanied it.

The black had recognized Tarzan as the white devil from the descriptions given by the whites and their black servants. Behind him he had expected to see a horde of demons disguised as apes and panthers.

In this Tarzan saw the cunning hand of Rokoff. The Russian was attempting to make travel as difficult as possible for him by turning the natives against him in superstitious fear.

The native further told Tarzan that the white man who had led the recent expedition had promised them a fabulous reward if they would kill the white devil. This they had fully intended doing should the opportunity present itself; but the moment they had seen Tarzan their blood had turned to water, as the porters of the white men had told them would be the case.

Finding the ape-man made no attempt to harm him, the native at last recovered his grasp upon his courage, and, at Tarzan's suggestion, accompanied the white devil back to the village, calling as he went for his fellows to return also, as "the white devil has promised to do you no harm if you come back right away and answer his questions."

One by one the blacks straggled into the village, but that their fears were not entirely allayed was evident from the amount of white that showed about the eyes of the majority of them as they cast constant and apprehensive sidelong glances at the ape-man.

The chief was among the first to return to the village, and as it was he that Tarzan was most anxious to interview, he lost no time in entering into a palaver with the black.

The fellow was short and stout, with an unusually low and degraded countenance and apelike arms. His whole expression denoted deceitfulness.

Only the superstitious terror engendered in him by the stories poured into his ears by the whites and blacks of the Russian's party kept him from leaping upon Tarzan with his warriors and slaying him forthwith, for he and his people were inveterate maneaters. But the fear that he might indeed be a devil, and that out there in the jungle behind him his fierce demons waited to do his bidding, kept M'ganwazam from putting his desires into action.

Tarzan questioned the fellow closely, and by comparing his statements with those of the young warrior he had first talked with he learned that Rokoff and his *safari* were in terror-stricken retreat in the direction of the far East Coast.

Many of the Russian's porters had already deserted him. In that very village he had hanged five for theft and attempted desertion. Judging, however, from what the Waganwazam had learned from those of the Russian's blacks who were not too far gone in terror of the brutal Rokoff to fear even to speak of their plans, it was apparent that he would not travel any great distance before the last of his porters, cooks, tent-boys, gun-bearers, *askari,* and even his headman, would have turned back into the bush, leaving him to the mercy of the merciless jungle.

M'ganwazam denied that there had been any white woman or child with the party of whites; but even as he spoke Tarzan was convinced that he lied. Several times the ape-man approached the subject from different angles, but never was he successful in surprising the wily cannibal into a direct contradiction of his original statement that there had been no women or children with the party.

Tarzan demanded food of the chief, and after considerable haggling on the part of the monarch succeeded in obtaining a meal. He then tried to draw out others of the tribe, especially the young man whom he had captured in the bush, but M'gazwazam's presence sealed their lips.

At last, convinced that these people knew a great deal more than they had told him concerning the whereabouts of the Russian and the fate of Jane and the child, Tarzan determined to remain overnight among them in the hope of discovering something further of importance.

When he had stated his decision to the chief he was

rather surprised to note the sudden change in the fellow's attitude toward him. From apparent dislike and suspicion M'ganwazam became a most eager and solicitous host.

Nothing would do but that the ape-man should occupy the best hut in the village, from which M'ganwazam's oldest wife was forthwith summarily ejected, while the chief took up his temporary abode in the hut of one of his younger consorts.

Had Tarzan chanced to recall the fact that a princely reward had been offered the blacks if they should succeed in killing him, he might have more quickly interpreted M'ganwazam's sudden change in front.

To have the white giant sleeping peacefully in one of his own huts would greatly facilitate the matter of earning the reward, and so the chief was urgent in his suggestions that Tarzan, doubtless being very much fatigued after his travels, should retire early to the comforts of the anything but inviting palace.

As much as the ape-man detested the thought of sleeping within a native hut, he had determined to do so this night, on the chance that he might be able to induce one of the younger men to sit and chat with him before the fire that burned in the centre of the smoke-filled dwelling, and from him draw the truths he sought. So Tarzan accepted the invitation of old M'ganwazam, insisting, however, that he much preferred sharing a hut with some of the younger men rather than driving the chief's old wife out in the cold.

The toothless old hag grinned her appreciation of this suggestion, and as the plan still better suited the chief's scheme, in that it would permit him to surround Tarzan with a gang of picked assassins, he readily assented, so that presently Tarzan had been installed in a hut close to the village gate.

As there was to be a dance that night in honour of a band of recently returned hunters, Tarzan was left alone in the hut, the young men, as M'ganwazam explained, having to take part in the festivities.

As soon as the ape-man was safely installed in the trap, M'ganwazam called about him the young warriors whom he had selected to spend the night with the white devil!

None of them was overly enthusiastic about the plan, since deep in their superstitious hearts lay an exaggerated fear of the strange white giant; but the word of M'ganwazam was law among his people, so not one dared refuse the duty he was called upon to perform.

As M'ganwazam unfolded his plan in whispers to the

savages squatting about him the old, toothless hag, to whom Tarzan had saved her hut for the night, hovered about the conspirators ostensibly to replenish the supply of firewood for the blaze about which the men sat, but really to drink in as much of their conversation as possible.

Tarzan had slept for perhaps an hour or two despite the savage din of the revellers when his keen senses came suddenly alert to a suspiciously stealthy movement in the hut in which he lay. The fire had died down to a little heap of glowing embers, which accentuated rather than relieved the darkness that shrouded the interior of the evil-smelling dwelling, yet the trained senses of the ape-man warned him of another presence creeping almost silently toward him through the gloom.

He doubted that it was one of his hut mates returning from the festivities, for he still heard the wild cries of the dancers and the din of the tom-toms in the village street without. Who could it be that took such pains to conceal his approach?

As the presence came within reach of him the ape-man bounded lightly to the opposite side of the hut, his spear poised ready at his side.

"Who is it," he asked, "that creeps upon Tarzan of the Apes, like a hungry lion out of the darkness?"

"Silence, *bwana!*" replied an old cracked voice. "It is Tambudza—she whose hut you would not take, and thus drive an old woman out into the cold night."

"What does Tambudza want of Tarzan of the Apes?" asked the ape-man.

"You were kind to me to whom none is now kind, and I have come to warn you in payment of your kindness," answered the old hag.

"Warn me of what?"

"M'ganwazam has chosen the young men who are to sleep in the hut with you," replied Tambudza. "I was near as he talked with them, and heard him issuing his instructions to them. When the dance is run well into the morning they are to come to the hut.

"If you are awake they are to pretend that they have come to sleep, but if you sleep it is M'ganwazam's command that you be killed. If you are not then asleep they will wait quietly beside you until you do sleep, and then they will all fall upon you together and slay you. M'ganwazam is determined to win the reward the white man has offered."

"I had forgotten the reward," said Tarzan, half to himself, and then he added, "How may M'ganwazam hope to collect the reward now that the white men who are my enemies have left his country and gone he knows not where?"

"Oh, they have not gone far," replied Tambudza. "M'ganwazam knows where they camp. His runners could quickly overtake them—they move slowly."

'Where are they?" asked Tarzan.

"Do you wish to come to them?" asked Tambudza in way of reply.

Tarzan nodded.

"I cannot tell you where they lie so that you could come to the place yourself, but I could lead you to them, *bwana*."

In their interest in the conversation neither of the speakers had noticed the little figure which crept into the darkness of the hut behind them, nor did they see it when it slunk noiselessly out again.

It was little Buulaoo, the chief's son by one of his younger wives—a vindictive, degenerate little rascal who hated Tambudza, and was ever seeking opportunities to spy upon her and report her slightest breach of custom to his father.

"Come, then," said Tarzan quickly, "let us be on our way."

This Buuaoo did not hear, for he was already legging it up the village street to where his hideous sire guzzled native beer, and watched the evolutions of the frantic dancers leaping high in the air and cavorting wildly in their hysterical capers.

So it happened that as Tarzan and Tambudza sneaked warily from the village and melted into the Stygian darkness of the jungle two lithe runners took their way in the same direction, though by another trail.

When they had come sufficiently far from the village to make it safe for them to speak above a whisper, Tarzan asked the old woman if she had seen aught of a white woman and a little child.

"Yes, *bwana*," replied Tambudza, "there was a woman with them and a little child—a little white piccaninny. It died here in our village of the fever and they buried it!"

12

A Black Scoundrel

WHEN Jane Clayton regained consciousness she saw Anderssen standing over her, holding the baby in his arms. As her eyes rested upon them an expression of misery and horror overspread her countenance.

"What is the matter?" he asked. "You ban sick?"

"Where is my baby?" she cried, ignoring his questions. Anderssen held out the chubby infant, but she shook her head.

"It is not mine," she said. "You knew that it was not mine. You are a devil like the Russian."

Anderssen's blue eyes stretched in surprise.

"Not yours!" he exclaimed. "You tole me the kid aboard the *Kincaid* ban your kid."

"Not this one," replied Jane dully. "The other. Where is the other? There must have been two. I did not know about this one."

"There vasn't no other kid. Ay tank this ban yours. Ay am very sorry."

Anderssen fidgeted about, standing first on one foot and then upon the other. It was perfectly evident to Jane that he was honest in his protestations of ignorance of the true identity of the child.

Presently the baby commenced to crow, and bounce up and down in the Swede's arms, at the same time leaning forward with little hands out-reaching toward the young woman.

She could not withstand the appeal, and with a low cry she sprang to her feet and gathered the baby to her breast.

For a few minutes she wept silently, her face buried in the baby's soiled little dress. The first shock of disappointment that the tiny thing had not been her beloved Jack was giving way to a great hope that after all some miracle had occurred to snatch her baby from Rokoff's hands at the last instant before the *Kincaid* sailed from England.

Then, too, there was the mute appeal of this wee waif alone and unloved in the midst of the horrors of the savage jungle. It was this thought more than any other that had sent her mother's heart out to the innocent babe, while still she suffered from disappointment that she had been deceived in its identity.

"Have you no idea whose child this is?" she asked Anderssen.

The man shook his head.

"Not now," he said. "If he ain't ban your kid, Ay don' know whose kid he do ban. Rokoff said it was yours. Ay tank he tank so, too.

"What we do with it now? Ay can't go back to the *Kincaid*. Rokoff would have me shot; but you can go back. Ay take you to the sea, and then some of these black men they take you to the ship—eh?"

"No! no!" cried Jane. "Not for the world. I would rather die than fall into the hands of that man again. No, let us go on and take this poor little creature with us. If God is willing we shall be saved in one way or another."

So they again took up their flight through the wilderness, taking with them a half-dozen of the Mosulas to carry provisions and the tents that Anderssen had smuggled aboard the small boat in preparation for the attempted escape.

The days and nights of torture that the young woman suffered were so merged into one long, unbroken nightmare of hideousness that she soon lost all track of time. Whether they had been wandering for days or years she could not tell. The one bright spot in that eternity of fear and suffering was the little child whose tiny hands had long since fastened their softly groping fingers firmly about her heart.

In a way the little thing took the place and filled the aching void that the theft of her own baby had left. It could never be the same, of course, but yet, day by day, she found her mother-love enveloping the waif more closely until she sometimes sat with closed eyes lost in the sweet imagining that the little bundle of humanity at her breast was truly her own.

For some time their progress inland was extremely slow. Word came to them from time to time through natives passing from the coast on hunting excursions that Rokoff had not yet guessed the direction of their flight. This, and the desire to make the journey as light as possible for the gently bred woman, kept Anderssen to a slow advance of short and easy marches with many rests.

The Swede insisted upon carrying the child while they travelled, and in countless other ways did what he could to help Jane Clayton conserve her strength. He had been terribly chagrined on discovering the mistake he had made in the identity of the baby, but once the young woman became convinced that his motives were truly chivalrous she would not permit him longer to upbraid himself for the error that he could not by any means have avoided.

At the close of each day's march Anderssen saw to the erection of a comfortable shelter for Jane and the child. Her tent was always pitched in the most favourable location. The thorn *boma* round it was the strongest and most impregnable that the Mosula could construct.

Her food was the best that their limited stores and the rifle of the Swede could provide, but the thing that touched her heart the closest was the gentle consideration and courtesy which the man always accorded her.

That such nobility of character could lie beneath so repulsive an exterior never ceased to be a source of wonder and amazement to her, until at last the innate chivalry of the man, and his unfailing kindliness and sympathy transformed his appearance in so far as Jane was concerned until she saw only the sweetness of his character mirrored in his countenance.

They had commenced to make a little better progress when word reached them that Rokoff was but a few marches behind them, and that he had at last discovered the direction of their flight. It was then that Anderssen took to the river, purchasing a canoe from a chief whose village lay a short distance from the Ugambi upon the bank of a tributary.

Thereafter the little party of fugitives fled up the broad Ugambi, and so rapid had their flight become that they no longer received word of their pursuers. At the end of canoe navigation upon the river, they abandoned their canoe and took to the jungle. Here progress became at once arduous, slow, and dangerous.

The second day after leaving the Ugambi the baby fell ill with fever. Anderssen knew what the outcome must be, but he had not the heart to tell Jane Clayton the truth, for he had seen that the young woman had come to love the child almost as passionately as though it had been her own flesh and blood.

As the baby's condition precluded farther advance, Anderssen withdrew a little from the main trail he had been

following and built a camp in a natural clearing on the
bank of a little river.

Here Jane devoted her every moment to caring for the
tiny sufferer, and as though her sorrow and anxiety were not
all that she could bear, a further blow came with the sudden
announcement of one of the Mosula porters who had been
foraging in the jungle adjacent that Rokoff and his party
were camped quite close to them, and were evidently upon
their trail to this little nook which all had thought so excel-
lent a hiding-place.

This information could mean but one thing, and that
that they must break camp and fly onward regardless of the
baby's condition. Jane Clayton knew the traits of the Russian
well enough to be positive that he would separate her from
the child the moment that he recaptured them, and she knew
that separation would mean the immediate death of the
baby.

As they stumbled forward through the tangled vegetation
along an old and almost overgrown game trail the Mosula
porters deserted them one by one.

The men had been staunch enough in their devotion and
loyalty as long as they were in no danger of being overtaken
by the Russian and his party. They had heard, however, so
much of the atrocious disposition of Rokoff that they had
grown to hold him in mortal terror, and now that they knew
he was close upon them their timid hearts would fortify them
no longer, and as quickly as possible they deserted the three
whites.

Yet on and on went Anderssen and the girl. The Swede
went ahead, to hew a way through the brush where the path
was entirely overgrown, so that on this march it was necessary that the young woman carry the child.

All day they marched. Late in the afternoon they realized
that they had failed. Close behind them they heard the noise
of a large *safari* advancing along the trail which they had
cleared for their pursuers.

When it became quite evident that they must be overtaken
in a short time Anderssen hid Jane behind a large tree, covering her and the child with brush.

"There is a village about a mile farther on," he said to her.
"The Mosula told me its location before they deserted us. Ay
try to lead the Russian off your trail, then you go on to
the village. Ay tank the chief ban friendly to white men—
the Mosula tal me he ban. Anyhow, that was all we can do.

"After while you get chief to tak you down by the Mosula
village at the sea again, an' after a while a ship is sure to put

into the mouth of the Ugambi. Then you be all right. Gude-by an' gude luck to you, lady!"

"But where are you going, Sven?" asked Jane. "Why can't you hide here and go back to the sea with me?"

"Ay gotta tal the Russian you ban dead, so that he don't luke for you no more," and Anderssen grinned.

"Why can't you join me then after you have told him that?" insisted the girl.

Anderssen shook his head.

"Ay don't tank Ay join anybody any more after Ay tal the Russian you ban dead," he said.

"You don't mean that you think he will kill you?" asked Jane, and yet in her heart she knew that that was exactly what the great scoundrel would do in revenge for his having been thwarted by the Swede. Anderssen did not reply, other than to warn her to silence and point toward the path along which they had just come.

"I don't care," whispered Jane Clayton. "I shall not let you die to save me if I can prevent it in any way. Give me your revolver. I can use that, and together we may be able to hold them off until we can find some means of escape."

"It won't work, lady," replied Anderssen. "They would only get us both, and then Ay couldn't do you no good at all. Think of the kid, lady, and what it would be for you both to fall into Rokoff's hands again. For his sake you must do what Ay say. Here, take my rifle and ammunition; you may need them."

He shoved the gun and bandoleer into the shelter beside Jane. Then he was gone.

She watched him as he returned along the path to meet the oncoming *safari* of the Russian. Soon a turn in the trail hid him from view.

Her first impulse was to follow. With the rifle she might be of assistance to him, and, further, she could not bear the terrible thought of being left alone at the mercy of the fearful jungle without a single friend to aid her.

She started to crawl from her shelter with the intention of running after Anderssen as fast as she could. As she drew the baby close to her she glanced down into its little face.

How red it was! How unnatural the little thing looked. She raised the cheek to hers. It was fiery hot with fever!

With a little gasp of terror Jane Calyton rose to her feet in the jungle path. The rifle and bandoleer lay forgotten in the shelter beside her. Anderssen was forgotten, and Rokoff, and her great peril.

All that rioted through her fear-mad brain was the fearful

fact that this little, helpless child was stricken with the terrible jungle-fever, and that she was helpless to do aught to allay its sufferings—sufferings that were sure to come during ensuing intervals of partial consciousness.

Her one thought was to find some one who could help her—some woman who had had children of her own—and with the thought came recollection of the friendly village of which Anderssen had spoken. If she could but reach it—in time!

There was no time to be lost. Like a startled antelope she turned and fled up the trail in the direction Anderssen had indicated.

From far behind came the sudden shouting of men, the sound of shots, and then silence. She knew that Anderssen had met the Russian.

A half-hour later she stumbled, exhausted, into a little thatched village. Instantly she was surrounded by men, women, and children. Eager, curious, excited natives plied her with a hundred questions, no one of which she could understand or answer.

All that she could do was to point tearfully at the baby, now wailing piteously in her arms, and repeat over and over, "Fever—fever—fever."

The blacks did not understand her words, but they saw the cause of her trouble, and soon a young woman had pulled her into a hut and with several others was doing her poor best to quiet the child and allay its agony.

The witch doctor came and built a little fire before the infant, upon which he boiled some strange concoction in a small earthen pot, making weird passes above it and mumbling strange, monotonous chants. Presently he dipped a zebra's tail into the brew, and with further mutterings and incantations sprinkled a few drops of the liquid over the baby's face.

After he had gone the women sat about and moaned and wailed until Jane thought that she should go mad; but, knowing that they were doing it all out of the kindness of their hearts, she endured the frightful waking nightmare of those awful hours in dumb and patient suffering.

It must have been well toward midnight that she became conscious of a sudden commotion in the village. She heard the voices of the natives raised in controversy, but she could not understand the words.

Presently she heard footsteps approaching the hut in which she squatted before a bright fire with the baby on her lap. The little thing lay very still now, its lids, half-raised, showed the pupils horribly upturned.

Jane Clayton looked into the little face with fear-haunted eyes. It was not her baby—not her flesh and blood—but how close, how dear the tiny, helpless thing had become to her. Her heart, bereft of its own, had gone out to this poor, little, nameless waif, and lavished upon it all the love that had been denied her during the long, bitter weeks of her captivity aboard the *Kincaid*.

She saw that the end was near, and though she was terrified at contemplation of her loss, still she hoped that it would come quickly now and end the sufferings of the little victim.

The footsteps she had heard without the hut now halted before the door. There was a whispered colloquy, and a moment later M'ganwazam, chief of the tribe, entered. She had seen but little of him, as the women had taken her in hand almost as soon as she had entered the village.

M'ganwazam, she now saw, was an evil-appearing savage with every mark of brutal degeneracy writ large upon his bestial countenance. To Jane Clayton he looked more gorilla than human. He tried to converse with her, but without success, and finally he called to some one without.

In answer to his summons another Negro entered—a man of very different appearance from M'ganwazam—so different, in fact, that Jane Clayton immediately decided that he was of another tribe. This man acted as interpreter, and almost from the first question that M'ganwazam put to her, Jane felt an intuitive conviction that the savage was attempting to draw information from her for some ulterior motive.

She thought it strange that the fellow should so suddenly have become interested in her plans, and especially in her intended destination when her journey had been interrupted at his village.

Seeing no reason for withholding the information, she told him the truth; but when he asked if she expected to meet her husband at the end of her trip, she shook her head negatively.

Then he told her the purpose of his visit, talking through the interpreter.

"I have just learned," he said, "from some men who live by the side of the great water, that your husband followed you up the Ugambi for several marches, when he was at last set upon by natives and killed. Therefore I have told you this that you might not waste your time in a long journey if you expected to meet your husband at the end of it; but instead could turn and retrace your steps to the coast."

Jane thanked M'ganwazam for his kindness, though her heart was numb with suffering at this new blow. She who had suffered so much was at last beyond reach of the keenest of misery's pangs, for her senses were numbed and calloused.

With bowed head she sat staring with unseeing eyes upon the face of the baby in her lap. M'ganwazam had left the hut. Sometime later she heard a noise at the entrance— another had entered. One of the women sitting opposite her threw a faggot upon the dying embers of the fire between them.

With a sudden flare it burst into renewed flame, lighting up the hut's interior as though by magic.

The flame disclosed to Jane Clayton's horrified gaze that the baby was quite dead. How long it had been so she could not guess.

A choking lump rose to her throat, her head drooped in silent misery upon the little bundle that she had caught suddenly to her breast.

For a moment the silence of the hut was unbroken. Then the native woman broke into a hideous wail.

A man coughed close before Jane Clayton and spoke her name.

With a start she raised her eyes to look into the sardonic countenance of Nikolas Rokoff.

13

Escape

FOR a moment Rokoff stood sneering down upon Jane Clayton, then his eyes fell to the little bundle in her lap. Jane had drawn one corner of the blanket over the child's face, so that to one who did not know the truth it seemed but to be sleeping.

"You have gone to a great deal of unnecessary trouble," said Rokoff, "to bring the child to this village. If you had attended to your own affairs I should have brought it here myself.

"You would have been spared the dangers and fatigue of the journey. But I suppose I must thank you for relieving me of the inconvenience of having to care for a young infant on the march.

"This is the village to which the child was destined from the first. M'ganwazam will rear him carefully, making a good cannibal of him, and if you ever chance to return to civilization it will doubtless afford you much food for thought as you compare the luxuries and comforts of your life with the details of the life your son is living in the village of the Waganwazam.

"Again I thank you for bringing him here for me, and now I must ask you to surrender him to me, that I may turn him over to his foster parents." As he concluded Rokoff held out his hands for the child, a nasty grin of vindictiveness upon his lips.

To his surprise Jane Clayton rose and, without a word of protest, laid the little bundle in his arms.

"Here is the child," she said. "Thank God he is beyond your power to harm."

Grasping the import of her words, Rokoff snatched the blanket from the child's face to seek confirmation of his fears. Jane Clayton watched his expression closely.

She had been puzzled for days for an answer to the question of Rokoff's knowledge of the child's identity. If she had been in doubt before the last shred of that doubt was wiped away as she witnessed the terrible anger of the Russian as he looked upon the dead face of the baby and realized that at the last moment his dearest wish for vengeance had been thwarted by a higher power.

Almost throwing the body of the child back into Jane Clayton's arms, Rokoff stamped up and down the hut, pounding the air with his clenched fists and cursing terribly. At last he halted in front of the young woman, bringing his face down close to hers.

"You are laughing at me," he shrieked. "You think that you have beaten me—eh? I'll show you, as I have shown the miserable ape you call 'husband,' what it means to interfere with the plans of Nikolas Rokoff.

"You have robbed me of the child. I cannot make him the son of a cannibal chief, but"—and he paused as though to let the full meaning of his threat sink deep—"I can make the mother the wife of a cannibal, and that I shall do—after I have finished with her myself."

If he had thought to wring from Jane Clayton any sign of terror he failed miserably. She was beyond that. Her brain and nerves were numb to suffering and shock.

To his surprise a faint, almost happy smile touched her lips. She was thinking with thankful heart that this poor little corpse was not that of her own wee Jack, and that—best of all—Rokoff evidently did not know the truth.

She would have liked to have flaunted the fact in his face, but she dared not. If he continued to believe that the child had been hers, so much safer would be the real Jack wherever he might be. She had, of course, no knowledge of the whereabouts of her little son—he did not know, even, that he still lived, and yet there was the chance that he might.

It was more than possible that without Rokoff's knowledge this child had been substituted for hers by one of the Russian's confederates, and that even now her son might be safe with friends in London, where there were many, both able and willing, to have paid any ransom which the traitorous conspirator might have asked for the safe release of Lord Greystoke's son.

She had thought it all out a hundred times since she had discovered that the baby which Anderssen had placed in her arms that night upon the *Kincaid* was not her own, and it had been a constant and growing source of happiness to her to dream the whole fantasy through in its every detail.

No, the Russian must never know that this was not her baby. She realized that her position was hopeless—with Anderssen and her husband dead there was no one in all the world with a desire to succour her who knew where she might be found.

Rokoff's threat, she realized, was no idle one. That he would do, or attempt to do, all that he had promised, she was perfectly sure; but at the worst it meant but a little earlier release from the hideous anguish that she had been enduring. She must find some way to take her own life before the Russian could harm her further.

Just now she wanted time—time to think and prepare herself for the end. She felt that she could not take the last, awful step until she had exhausted every possibility of escape. She did not care to live unless she might fine her way back to her own child, but slight as such a hope appeared she would not admit its impossibility until the last moment had come, and she faced the fearful reality of choosing between the final alternatives—Nikolas Rokoff on one hand and self-destruction upon the other.

"Go away!" she said to the Russian. "Go away and leave me in peace with my dead. Have you not brought sufficient misery and anguish upon me without attempting to harm me further? What wrong have I ever done you that you should persist in persecuting me?"

"You are suffering for the sins of the monkey you chose when you might have had the love of a gentleman—of Nikolas Rokoff", he replied. "But where is the use in discussing the matter? We shall bury the child here, and you will return with me at once to my own camp. Tomorrow I shall bring you back and turn you over to your new husband —the lovely M'ganwazam. Come!"

He reached out for the child. Jane, who was on her feet now, turned away from him.

"I shall bury the body," she said. "Send some men to dig a grave outside the village."

Rokoff was anxious to have the thing over and get back to his camp with his victim. He thought he saw in her apathy a resignation to her fate. Stepping outside the hut, he motioned her to follow him, and a moment later, with his men, he escorted Jane beyond the village, where beneath a great tree the blacks scooped a shallow grave.

Wrapping the tiny body in a blanket, Jane laid it tenderly in the black hole, and, turning her head that she might not see the mouldy earth falling upon the pitiful little bundle, she breathed a prayer beside the grave of the nameless waif that had won its way to the innermost recesses of her heart.

Then, dry-eyed but suffering, she rose and followed the Russian through the Stygian blackness of the jungle, along the winding, leafy corridor that led from the village of M'ganwazam, the black cannibal, to the camp of Nikolas Rokoff, the white fiend.

Beside them, in the impenetrable thickets that fringed the path, rising to arch above it and shut out the moon, the girl could hear the stealthy, muffled footfalls of great beasts, and ever round about them rose the deafening roars of hunting lions, until the earth trembled to the mighty sound.

The porters lighted torches now and waved them upon either hand to frighten off the beasts of prey. Rokoff urged them to greater speed, and from the quavering note in his voice Jane Clayton knew that he was weak from terror.

The sounds of the jungle night recalled most vividly the days and nights that she had spent in a smiliar jungle with her forest god—with the fearless and unconquerable Tarzan of the Apes. Then there had been no thoughts of terror, though the jungle noises were new to her, and the roar of a lion had seemed the most awe-inspiring sound upon the great earth.

How different would it be now if she knew that he was somewhere there in the wilderness, seeking her! Then, indeed, would there be that for which to live, and every reason to believe that succour was close at hand—but he was dead! It was incredible that it should be so.

There seemed no place in death for that great body and those mighty thews. Had Rokoff been the one to tell her of her lord's passing she would have known that he lied. There could be no reason, she thought, why M'ganwazam should have deceived her. She did not know that the Russian had talked with the savage a few minutes before the chief had come to her with his tale.

At last they reached the rude *boma* that Rokoff's porters had thrown up round the Russian's camp. Here they found all in turmoil. She did not know what it was all about, but she saw that Rokoff was very angry, and from bits of conversation which she could translate she gleaned that there had been further desertions while he had been absent, and that the deserters had taken the bulk of his food and ammunition.

When he had done venting his rage upon those who remained he returned to where Jane stood under guard of a couple of his white sailors. He grasped her roughly by the arm and started to drag her toward his tent. The girl struggled and fought to free herself, while the two sailors stood by, laughing at the rare treat.

Rokoff did not hesitate to use rough methods when he found that he was to have difficulty in carrying out his designs. Repeatedly he struck Jane Clayton in the face, until at last, half-conscious, she was dragged within his tent.

Rokoff's boy had lighted the Russian's lamp, and now at a word from his master he made himself scarce. Jane had sunk to the floor in the middle of the enclosure. Slowly her numbed senses were returning to her and she was commencing to think very fast indeed. Quickly her eyes ran round the interior of the tent, taking in every detail of its equipment and contents.

Now the Russian was lifting her to her feet and attempting to drag her to the camp cot that stood at one side of the tent. At his belt hung a heavy revolver. Jane Clayton's eyes riveted themselves upon it. Her palm itched to grasp the huge butt. She feigned again to swoon, but through her half-closed lids she waited her opportunity.

It came just as Rokoff was lifting her upon the cot. A noise at the tent door behind him brought his head quickly about and away from the girl. The butt of the gun was not an inch from her hand. With a single, lightning-like move she snatched the weapon from its holster, and at the same instant Rokoff turned back toward her, realizing his peril.

She did not dare fire for fear the shot would bring his people about him, and with Rokoff dead she would fall into hands no better than his and to a fate probably even worse than he alone could have imagined. The memory of the two brutes who stood and laughed as Rokoff struck her was still vivid.

As the rage and fear-filled countenance of the Slav turned toward her Jane Clayton raised the heavy revolver high above the pasty face and with all her strength dealt the man a terrific blow between the eyes.

Without a sound he sank, limp and unconscious, to the ground. A moment later the girl stood beside him—for a moment at least free from the menace of his lust.

Outside the tent she again heard the noise that had distracted Rokoff's attention. What it was she did not know, but, fearing the return of the servant and the discovery of her deed, she stepped quickly to the camp table upon which burned the oil lamp and extinguished the smudgy, evil-smelling flame.

In the total darkness of the interior she paused for a moment to collect her wits and plan for the next step in her venture for freedom.

About her was a camp of enemies. Beyond these foes a black wilderness of savage jungle peopled by hideous beasts of prey and still more hideous human beasts.

There was little or no chance that she could survive even a few days of the constant dangers that would confront her there; but the knowledge that she had already passed through so many perils unscathed, and that somewhere out in the faraway world a little child was doubtless at that very moment crying for her, filled her with determination to make the effort to accomplish the seemingly impossible and cross that awful land of horror in search of the sea and the remote chance of succour she might find there.

Rokoff's tent stood almost exactly in the centre of the *boma*. Surrounding it were the tents and shelters of his white companions and the natives of his *safari*. To pass through these and find egress through the *boma* seemed a task too fraught with insurmountable obstacles to warrant even the slightest consideration, and yet there was no other way.

To remain in the tent until she should be discovered would be to set at naught all that she had risked to gain her free-dom, and so with stealthy step and every sense alert she approached the back of the tent to set out upon the first stage of her adventure.

Groping along the rear of the canvas wall, she found that there was no opening there. Quickly she returned to the side of the unconscious Russian. In his belt her groping fingers came upon the hilt of a long hunting-knife, and with this she cut a hole in the back wall of the tent.

Silently she stepped without. To her immense relief she saw that the camp was apparently asleep. In the dim and flickering light of the dying fires she saw but a single sentry, and he was dozing upon his haunches at the opposite side of the enclosure.

Keeping the tent between him and herself, she crossed between the small shelters of the native porters to the *boma* wall beyond.

Outside, in the darkness of the tangled jungle, she could hear the roaring of lions, the laughing of hyenas, and the countelss, nameless noises of the midnight jungle.

For a moment she hesitated, trembling. The thought of the prowling beasts out there in the darkness was appalling. Then, with a sudden brave toss of her head, she attacked the thorny *boma* wall with her delicate hands. Torn and bleeding though they were, she worked on breathlessly until she had made an opening through which she could worm her body, and at last she stood outside the enclosure.

Behind her lay a fate worse than death, at the hands of human beings.

Before her lay an almost certain fate—but it was only death—sudden, merciful, and honourable death.

Without a tremor and without regret she darted away from the camp, and a moment later the mysterious jungle had closed about her.

14

Alone in the Jungle

TAMBUDZA, leading Tarzan of the Apes toward the camp of the Russian, moved very slowly along the winding jungle path, for she was old and her legs tiff with rheumatism.

So it was that the runners dispatched by M'ganwazam to warn Rokoff that the white giant was in his village and that he would be slain that night reached the Russian's camp before Tarzan and his ancient guide had covered half the distance.

The guides found the white man's camp in a turmoil.

Rokoff had that morning been discovered stunned and bleeding within his tent. When he had recovered his senses and realized that Jane Clayton had escaped, his rage was boundless.

Rushing about the camp with his rifle, he had sought to shoot down the native sentries who had allowed the young woman to elude their vigilance, but several of the other whites, realizing that they were already in a precarious position owing to the numerous desertions that Rokoff's cruelty had brought about, seized and disarmed him.

Then came the messengers from M'ganwazam, but scarce had they told their story and Rokoff was preparing to depart with them for their village when other runners, panting from the exertions of their swift flight through the jungle, rushed breathless into the firelight, crying that the great white giant had escaped from M'ganwazam and was already on his way to wreak vengeance against his enemies.

Instantly confusion reigned within the encircling *boma*. The blacks belonging to Rokoff's *safari* were terror-stricken at the thought of the proximity of the white giant who hunted through the jungle with a fierce pack of apes and panthers at his heels.

Before the whites realized what had happened the superstitious fears of the natives had sent them scurrying into the bush—their own carriers as well as the messengers from M'ganwazam—but even in their haste they had not neglected to take with them every article of value upon which they could lay their hands.

Thus Rokoff and the seven white sailors found themselves deserted and robbed in the midst of a wilderness.

The Russian, following his usual custom, berated his companions, laying all the blame upon their shoulders for the events which had led up to the almost hopeless condition in which they now found themselves; but the sailors were in no mood to brook his insults and his cursing.

In the midst of this tirade one of them drew a revolver and fired point-blank at the Russian. The fellow's aim was poor, but his act so terrified Rokoff that he turned and fled for his tent.

As he ran his eyes chanced to pass beyond the *boma* to the edge of the forest, and there he caught a glimpse of that which sent his craven heart cold with a fear that almost expunged his terror of the seven men at his back, who by this time were all firing in hate and revenge at his retreating figure.

What he saw was the giant figure of an almost naked white man emerging from the bush.

Darting into his tent, the Russian did not halt in his flight, but kept right on through the rear wall, taking advantage of the long slit that Jane Clayton had made the night before.

The terror-stricken Muscovite scurried like a hunted rabbit through the hole that still gaped in the *boma's* wall at the point where his own prey had escaped, and as Tarzan approached the camp upon the opposite side Rokoff disappeared into the jungle in the wake of Jane Clayton.

As the ape-man entered the *boma* with old Tambudza at his elbow the seven sailors, recognizing him, turned and fled in the opposite direction. Tarzan saw that Rokoff was not among them, and so he let them go their way—his business was with the Russian, whom he expected to find in his tent. As to the sailors, he was sure that the jungle would exact from them expiation for their villainies, nor, doubtless, was he wrong, for his were the last white man's eyes to rest upon any of them.

Finding Rokoff's tent empty, Tarzan was about to set out in search of the Russian when Tambudza suggested to him that the departure of the white man could only have resulted from word reaching him from M'ganwazam that Tarzan was in his village.

"He has doubtless hastened there," argued the old woman. "If you would find him let us return at once."

Tarzan himself thought that this would probably prove to be the fact, so he did not waste time in an endeavour to locate the Russian's trail, but, instead, set out briskly for the village of M'ganwazam, leaving Tambudza to plod slowly in his wake.

His one hope was that Jane was still safe and with Rokoff. If this was the case, it would be but a matter of an hour or more before he should be able to wrest her from the Russian.

He knew now that M'ganwazam was treacherous and that he might have to fight to regain possession of his wife. He wished that Mugambi, Sheeta, Akut, and the balance of the pack were with him, for he realized that single-handed it would be no child's play to bring Jane safely from the clutches of two such scoundrels as Rokoff and the wily M'ganwazam.

To his surprise he found no sign of either Rokoff or Jane in the village, and as he could not trust the word of the chief, he wasted no time in futile inquiry. So sudden and unexpected had been his return, and so quickly had he vanished into the jungle after learning that those he sought were not among the Waganwazam, that old M'ganwazam had no time to prevent his going.

Swinging through the trees, he hastened back to the deserted camp he had so recently left, for here, he knew, was the logical place to take up the trail of Rokoff and Jane.

Arrived at the *boma,* he circled carefully about the outside of the enclosure until, opposite a break in the thorny wall, he came to indications that something had recently passed into the jungle. His acute sense of smell told him that both of those he sought had fled from the camp in this direction, and a moment later he had taken up the trail and was following the faint spoor.

Far ahead of him a terror-stricken young woman was slinking along a narrow game-trail, fearful that the next moment would bring her face to face with some savage beast or equally savage man. As she ran on, hoping against hope that she had hit upon the direction that would lead her eventually to the great river, she came suddenly upon a familiar spot.

At one side of the trail, beneath a giant tree, lay a little heap of loosely piled brush—to her dying day that little spot of jungle would be indelibly impressed upon her memory. It was where Anderssen had hidden her—where he had given up his life in the vain effort to save her from Rokoff.

At sight of it she recalled the rifle and ammunition that the man had thrust upon her at the last moment. Until now she had forgotten them entirely. Still clutched in her hand was the revolver she had snatched from Rokoff's belt, but that could contain at most not over six cartridges—not enough to furnish her with food and protection both on the long journey to the sea.

With bated breath she groped beneath the little mound, scarce daring to hope that the treasure remained where she had left it; but, to her infinite relief and joy, her hand came at once upon the barrel of the heavy weapon and then upon the bandoleer of cartridges.

As she threw the latter about her shoulder and felt the weight of the big game-gun in her hand a sudden sense of security suffused her. It was with new hope and a feeling almost of assured success that she again set forward upon her journey.

That night she slept in the crotch of a tree, as Tarzan had so often told her that he was accustomed to doing, and early the next morning was upon her way again. Late in the afternoon, as she was about to cross a little clearing, she was startled at sight of a huge ape coming from the jungle upon the opposite side.

The wind was blowing directly across the clearing between them, and Jane lost no time in putting herself downwind from the huge creature. Then she hid in a clump of heavy bush and watched, holding the rifle ready for instant use.

Slowly the monster advanced across the clearing, sniffing at the ground from time to time, as though following spoor by scent. Scarcely had the great anthropoid taken a dozen steps into the clearing before another of his kind followed from the jungle, and then another and another, until five of the ferocious beasts were in plain sight of the terrified girl crouching in her hiding-place with the heavy rifle ready for instant use.

To her consternation she saw that the apes were pausing in the centre of the clearing. They came together in a little knot, where they stood looking backward, as though in expectation of the coming of others of their tribe.

Jane wished that they would go on, for she knew that at any moment some little, eddying gust of wind might carry her scent down to their nostrils, and then what would the protection of her rifle amount to in the face of those gigantic muscles and mighty fangs?

Her eyes moved back and forth between the apes and the edge of the jungle toward which they were gazing until at last she perceived the object of their halt and the thing that they awaited. They were being stalked.

Of this she was positive, as she saw the lithe, sinewy form of a panther glide noiselessly from the jungle at the point at which the apes had emerged but a moment before.

Quickly the beast trotted across the clearing toward the anthropoids. Jane wondered at their apparent apathy, and a moment later her wonder turned to amazement as she saw the great cat come quite close to the apes, who appeared entirely unconcerned by its presence, and, squatting down in their midst, fell assiduously to the business of preening, which occupies most of the waking hours of the cat family.

If the young woman was surprised by the sight of these natural enemies fraternizing, it was with emotions little short of fear for her own sanity that she presently saw a tall, muscular warrior enter the clearing and join the group of savage beasts assembled there.

At first sight of the man she had been positive that he would be torn to pieces, and she had half risen from her shelter, raising her rifle to her shoulder to do what she could to avert the man's terrible fate.

Now she saw that he seemed actually conversing with the beasts—issuing orders to them.

Presently the entire company filed on across the clearing and disappeared in the jungle upon the opposite side.

With a gasp of mingled incredulity and relief Jane Clayton staggered to her feet and fled on away from the terrible horde that had just passed her, while a half-mile behind her another individual, following the same trail as she, lay frozen with terror behind an ant-hill as the hideous band passed quite close to him.

This one was Rokoff; but he had recognized the members of the awful aggregation as allies of Tarzan of the Apes. No sooner, therefore, had the beasts passed him than he rose and raced through the jungle as fast as he could go, in order that he might put as much distance as possible between himself and these frightful beasts.

So it happened that as Jane Clayton came to the bank of the river, down which she hoped to float to the ocean and eventual rescue, Nikolas Rokoff was but a short distance in her rear.

Upon the bank the girl saw a great dugout drawn half-way from the water and tied securely to a near-by tree.

This, she felt, would solve the question of transportation to the sea could she but launch the huge, unwieldy craft. Unfastening the rope that had moored it to the tree, Jane pushed frantically upon the bow of the heavy canoe, but for all the results that were apparent she might as well have been attempting to shove the earth out of its orbit.

She was about winded when it occurred to her to try working the dugout into the stream by loading the stern with ballast and then rocking the bow back and forth along the bank until the craft eventually worked itself into the river.

There were no stones or rocks available, but along the shore she found quantities of driftwood deposited by the river at a slightly higher stage. These she gathered and piled far in the stern of the boat, until at last, to her immense relief, she saw the bow rise gently from the mud of the bank and the stern drift slowly with the current until it again lodged a few feet farther sown-stream.

Jane found that by running back and forth between the bow and stern she could alternately raise and lower each end of the boat as she shifted her weight from one end to the other, with the result that each time she leaped to the stern the canoe moved a few inches farther into the river.

As the success of her plan approached more closely to fruition she became so wrapped in her efforts that she failed to note the figure of a man standing beneath a huge tree at the edge of the jungle from which he had just emerged.

He watched her and her labours with a cruel and malicious grin upon his swarthy countenance.

The boat at last became so nearly free of the retarding

mud and of the bank that Jane felt positive that she could pole it off into deeper water with one of the paddles which lay in the bottom of the rude craft. With this end in view she seized upon one of these implements and had just plunged it into the river bottom close to the shore when her eyes happened to rise to the edge of the jungle.

As her gaze fell upon the figure of the man a little cry of terror rose to her lips. It was Rokoff.

He was running toward her now and shouting to her to wait or he would shoot—though he was entirely unarmed it was difficult to discover just how he intended making good his threat.

Jane Clayton knew nothing of the various misfortunes that had befallen the Russian since she had escaped from his tent, so she believed that his followers must be close hand.

However, she had no intention of falling again into the man's clutches. She would rather die at once than that that should happen her. Another minute and the boat would be free.

Once in the current of the river she would be beyond Rokoff's power to stop her, for there was no other boat upon the shore, and no man, and certainly not the cowardly Rokoff, would dare to attempt to swim the crocodile-infested water in an effort to overtake her.

Rokoff, on his part, was bent more upon escape than aught else. He would gladly have forgone any designs he might have had upon Jane Clayton would she but permit him to share this means of escape that she had discovered. He would promise anything if she would let him come aboard the dugout, but he did not think that it was necessary to do so.

He saw that he could easily reach the bow of the boat before it cleared the shore, and then it would not be necessary to make promises of any sort. Not that Rokoff would have felt the slightest compunction in ignoring any promises he might have made the girl, but he disliked the idea of having to sue for favour with one who had so recently assaulted and escaped him.

Already he was gloating over the days and nights of revenge that would be his while the heavy dugout drifted its slow way to the ocean.

Jane Clayton, working furiously to shove the boat beyond his reach, suddenly realized that she was to be successful, for with a little lurch the dugout swung quickly into the current, just as the Russian reached out to place his hand upon its bow.

His fingers did not miss their goal by a half-dozen inches. The girl almost collapsed with the reaction from the terrific mental, physical, and nervous strain under which she had been labouring for the past few minutes. But, thank Heaven, at last she was safe!

Even as she breathed a silent prayer of thanksgiving, she saw a sudden expression of triumph lighten the features of the cursing Russian, and at the same instant he dropped suddenly to the ground, grasping firmly upon something which wriggled through the mud toward the water.

Jane Clayton crouched, wide-eyed and horror-stricken, in the bottom of the boat as she realized that at the last instant success had been turned to failure, and that she was indeed again in the power of the malignant Rokoff.

For the thing that the man had seen and grasped was the end of the trailing rope with which the dugout had been moored to the tree.

15

Down the Ugambi

HALF-WAY between the Ugambi and the village of the Waganwazam, Tarzan came upon the pack moving slowly along his old spoor. Mugambi could scarce believe that the trail of the Russian and the mate of his savage master had passed so close to that of the pack.

It seemed incredible that two human beings should have come so close to them without having been detected by some of the marvellously keen and alert beasts; but Tarzan pointed out the spoor of the two he trailed, and at certain points the black could see that the man and the woman must have been in hiding as the pack passed them, watching every move of the ferocious creatures.

It had been apparent to Tarzan from the first that Jane and Rokoff were not travelling together. The spoor showed distinctly that the young woman had been a considerable distance ahead of the Russian at first, though the farther the ape-man continued along the trail the more obvious it became that the man was rapidly overhauling his quarry.

At first there had been the spoor of wild beasts over the footprints of Jane Clayton, while upon the top of all Rokoff's spoor showed that he had passed over the trail after the animals had left their records upon the ground. But later there were fewer and fewer animal imprints occurring between those of Jane's and the Russian's feet, until as he approached the river the ape-man became aware that Rokoff could not have been more than a few hundred yards behind the girl.

He felt they must be close ahead of him now, and, with a little thrill of expectation, he leaped rapidly forward ahead of the pack. Swinging swiftly through the trees, he came out upon the river-bank at the very point at which Rokoff had overhauled Jane as she endeavoured to launch the cumbersome dugout.

In the mud along the bank the ape-man saw the footprints of the two he sought, but there was neither boat nor people there when he arrived, nor, at first glance, any sign of their whereabouts.

It was plain that they had shoved off a native canoe and embarked upon the bosom of the stream, and as the ape-man's eye ran swiftly down the course of the river beneath the shadows of the overarching trees he saw in the distance, just as it rounded a bend that shut it off from his view, a drifting dugout in the stern of which was the figure of a man.

Just as the pack came in sight of the river they saw their agile leader racing down the river's bank, leaping from hummock to hummock of the swampy ground that spread between them and a little promontory which rose just where the river curved inward from their sight.

To follow him it was necessary for the heavy, cumbersome apes to make a wide detour, and Sheeta, too, who hated water. Mugambi followed after them as rapidly as he could in the wake of the great white master.

A half-hour of rapid travelling across the swampy neck of land and over the rising promontory brought Tarzan, by a short cut, to the inward bend of the winding river, and there before him upon the bosom of the stream he saw the dugout, and in its stern Nikolas Rokoff.

Jane was not with the Russian.

At sight of his enemy the broad scar upon the ape-man's brow burned scarlet, and there rose to his lips the hideous, bestial challenge of the bull-ape.

Rokoff shuddered as the weird and terrible alarm fell upon his ears. Cowering in the bottom of the boat, his teeth chattering in terror, he watched the man he feared above all other creatures upon the face of the earth as he ran quickly to the edge of the water.

Even though the Russian knew that he was safe from his enemy, the very sight of him threw him into a frenzy of trembling cowardice, which became frantic hysteria as he saw the white giant dive fearlessly into the forbidding waters of the tropical river.

With steady, powerful strokes the ape-man forged out into the stream toward the drifting dugout. Now Rokoff seized one of the paddles lying in the bottom of the craft, and, with terrorwide eyes still glued upon the living death that pursued him, struck out madly in an effort to augment the speed of the unwieldy canoe.

And from the opposite bank a sinister ripple, unseen by either man, moving steadily toward the half-naked swimmer.

Tarzan had reached the stern of the craft at last. One hand upstretched grasped the gunwale. Rokoff sat frozen with fear, unable to move a hand or foot, his eyes riveted upon the face of his Nemesis.

Then a sudden commotion in the water behind the swimmer caught his attention. He saw the ripple, and he knew what caused it.

At the same instant Tarzan felt mighty jaws close upon his right leg. He tried to struggle free and raise himself over the side of the boat. His efforts would have succeeded had not this unexpected interruption galvanized the malign brain of the Russian into instant action with its sudden promise of deliverance and revenge.

Like a venomous snake the man leaped toward the stern of the boat, and with a single swift blow struck Tarzan across the head with the heavy paddle. The ape-man's fingers slipped from their hold upon the gunwale.

There was a short struggle at the surface, and then a swirl of waters, a little eddy, and a burst of bubbles soon smoothed out by the flowing current marked for the instant the spot where Tarzan of the Apes, Lord of the Jungle, disappeared from the sight of men beneath the gloomy waters of the dark and forbidding Ugambi.

Weak from terror, Rokoff sank shuddering into the bottom of the dugout. For a moment he could not realize the good fortune that had befallen him—all that he could see was the figure of a silent, struggling white man disappearing beneath the surface of the river to unthinkable death in the slimy mud of the bottom.

Slowly all that it meant to him filtered into the mind of the Russian, and then a cruel smile of relief and triumph touched his lips; but it was short-lived, for just as he was

congratulating himself that he was now comparatively safe to
proceed upon his way to the coast unmolested, a mighty pandemonium rose from the river-bank close by.

As his eyes sought the authors of the frightful sound he
saw standing upon the shore, glaring at him with hate-
filled eyes, a devil-faced panther surrounded by the hideous
apes of Akut, and in the forefront of them a giant black
warrior who shook his fist at him, threatening him with
terrible death.

The nightmare of that flight down the Ugambi with the
hideous horde racing after him by day and by night, now
abreast of him, now lost in the mazes of the jungle far behind for hours and once for a whole day, only to appear
again upon his trail grim, relentless, and terrible, reduced
the Russian from a strong and robust man to an emaciated,
white-haired, fear-gibbering thing or ever the bay and the
ocean broke upon his hopeless vision.

Past populous villages he had fled. Time and again
warriors had put out in their canoes to intercept him, but
each time the hideous horde had swept into view to send the
terrified natives shrieking back to the shore to lose themselves in the jungle.

Nowhere in his flight had he seen aught of Jane Clayton.
Not once had his eyes rested upon her since that moment
at the river's brim his hand had closed upon the rope at-
tached to the bow of her dugout and he had believed her
safely in his power again, only to be thwarted an instant
later as the girl snatched up a heavy express rifle from the
bottom of the craft and levelled it full at his breast.

Quickly he had dropped the rope then and seen her float
away beyond his reach, but a moment later he had been
racing up-stream toward a little tributary in the mouth of
which was hidden the canoe in which he and his party had
come thus far upon their journey in pursuit of the girl and
Anderssen.

What had become of her?

There seemed little doubt in the Russian's mind, however, but that she had been captured by warriors from one
of the several villages she would have been compelled to
pass on her way down to the sea. Well, he was at least rid
of most of his human enemies.

But at that he would gladly have had them all back in
the land of the living could he thus have been freed from
the menace of the frightful creatures who pursued him with
awful relentlessness, screaming and growling at him every
time they came within sight of him. The one that filled him
with the greatest terror was the panther—the flaming-eyed,

devil-faced panther whose grinning jaws gaped wide at him by day, and whose fiery orbs gleamed wickedly out across the water from the Cimmerian blackness of the jungle nights.

The sight of the mouth of the Ugambi filled Rokoff with renewed hope, for there, upon the yellow waters of the bay, floated the *Kincaid* at anchor. He had sent the little steamer away to coal while he had gone up the river, leaving Paulvitch in charge of her, and he could have cried aloud in his relief as he saw that she had returned in time to save him.

Frantically he alternately paddled furiously toward her and rose to his feet waving his paddle and crying aloud in an attempt to attract the attention of those on board. But loud as he screamed his cries awakened no answering challenge from the deck of the silent craft.

Upon the shore behind him a hurried backward glance revealed the presence of the snarling pack. Even now, he thought, these manlike devils might yet find a way to reach him even upon the deck of the steamer unless there were those there to repel them with firearms.

What could have happened to those he had left upon the *Kincaid?* Where was Paulvitch? Could it be that the vessel was deserted, and that, after all, he was doomed to be overtaken by the terrible fate that he had been flying from through all these hideous days and nights? He shivered as might one upon whose brow death has already laid his clammy finger.

Yet he did not cease to paddle frantically toward the steamer, and at last, after what seemed an eternity, the bow of the dugout bumped against the timbers of the *Kincaid*. Over the ship's side hung a monkey-ladder, but as the Russian grasped it to ascend to the deck he heard a warning challenge from above, and, looking up, gazed into the cold, relentless muzzle of a rifle.

After Jane Clayton, with rifle levelled at the breast of Rokoff, had succeeded in holding him off until the dugout in which she had taken refuge had drifted out upon the bosom of the Ugambi beyond the man's reach, she had lost no time in paddling to the swiftest sweep of the channel, nor did she for long days and weary nights cease to hold her craft to the most rapidly moving part of the river, except when during the hottest hours of the day she had been wont to drift as the current would take her, lying prone in the bottom of the canoe, her face sheltered from the sun with a great palm leaf.

Thus only did she gain rest upon the voyage; at other

times she continually sought to augment the movement of
the craft by wielding the heavy paddle.

Rokoff, on the other hand, had used little or no intelligence in his flight along the Ugambi, so that more often than
not his craft had drifted in the slow-going eddies, for he
habitually hugged the bank farthest from that along which
the hideous horde pursued and menaced him.

Thus it was that, though he had put out upon the river
but a short time subsequent to the girl, yet she had reached
the bay fully two hours ahead of him. When she had first
seen the anchored ship upon the quiet water, Jane Clayton's
heart had beat fast with hope and thanksgiving, but as she
drew closer to the craft and saw that it was the *Kincaid,*
her pleasure gave place to the gravest misgivings.

It was too late, however, to turn back, for the current that
carried her toward the ship was much too strong for her
muscles. She could not have forced the heavy dugout up-
stream against it, and all that was left her was to attempt
either to make the shore without being seen by those upon
the deck of the *Kincaid,* or to throw herself upon their
mercy—otherwise she must be swept out to sea.

She knew that the shore held little hope of life for her,
as she had no knowledge of the location of the friendly
Mosula village to which Anderssen had taken her through
the darkness of the night of their escape from the *Kincaid.*

With Rokoff away from the steamer it might be possible
that by offering those in charge a large reward they could
be induced to carry her to the nearest civilized port. It was
worth risking—if she could make the steamer at all.

The current was bearing her swiftly down the river, and
she found that only by dint of the utmost exertion could
she direct the awkward craft toward the vicinity of the
Kincaid. Having reached the decision to board the steamer,
she now looked to it for aid, but to her surprise the decks
appeared to be empty and she saw no sign of life aboard
the ship.

The dugout was drawing closer and closer to the bow of
the vessel, and yet no hail came over the side from any
lookout aboard. In a moment more, Jane realized, she
would be swept beyond the steamer, and then, unless they
lowered a boat to rescue her, she would be carried far out
to sea by the current and the swift ebb tide that was running.

The young woman called loudly for assistance, but there
was no reply other than the shrill scream of some savage
beast upon the jungle-shrouded shore. Frantically Jane

wielded the paddle in an effort to carry her craft close alongside the steamer.

For a moment it seemed that she should miss her goal by but a few feet, but at the last moment the canoe swung close beneath the steamer's bow and Jane barely managed to grasp the anchor chain.

Heroically she clung to the heavy iron links, almost dragged from the canoe by the strain of the current upon her craft. Beyond her she saw a monkey-ladder dangling over the steamer's side. To release her hold upon the chain and chance clambering to the ladder as her canoe was swept beneath it seemed beyond the pale of possibility, yet to remain clinging to the anchor chain appeared equally as futile.

Finally her glance chanced to fall upon the rope in the bow of the dugout, and, making one end of this fast to the chain, she succeeded in drifting the canoe slowly down until it lay directly beneath the ladder. A moment later, her rifle slung about her shoulders, she had clambered safely to the deserted deck.

Her first task was to explore the ship, and this she did, her rifle ready for instant use stould she meet with any human menace aboard the *Kincaid*. She was not long in discovering the cause of the apparently deserted condition of the steamer, for in the forecastle she found the sailors, who had evidently been left to guard the ship, deep in drunken slumber.

With a shudder of disgust she clambered above, and to the best of her ability closed and made fast the hatch above the heads of the sleeping guard. Next she sought the galley and food, and, having appeased her hunger, she took her place on deck, determined that none should board the *Kincaid* without first having agreed to her demands.

For an hour or so nothing appeared upon the surface of the river to cause her alarm, but then, about a bend upstream, she saw a canoe appear in which sat a single figure. It had not proceeded far in her direction before she recognized the occupant as Rokoff, and when the fellow attempted to board he found a rifle staring him in the face.

When the Russian discovered who it was that repelled his advance he became furious, cursing and threatening in a most horrible manner; but, finding that these tactics failed to frighten or move the girl, he at last fell to pleading and promising.

Jane had but a single reply for his every proposition, and that was that nothing would ever persuade her to permit Rokoff upon the same vessel with her. That she would put her threats into action and shoot him should he persist in his endeavour to board the ship he was convinced.

So, as there was no other alternative, the great coward dropped back into his dugout and, at imminent risk of being swept to sea, finally succeeded in making the shore far down the bay and upon the opposite side from that on which the horde of beasts stood snarling and roaring.

Jane Clayton knew that the fellow could not alone and un-aided bring his heavy craft back up-stream to the *Kincaid*, and so she had no further fear of an attack by him. The hideous crew upon the shore she thought she recognized as the same that had passed her in the jungle far up the Ugambi several days before, for it seemed quite beyond reason that there should be more than one such a strangely assorted pack; but what had brought them down-stream to the mouth of the river she could not imagine.

Toward the day's close the girl was suddenly alarmed by the shouting of the Russian from the opposite bank of the stream, and a moment later, following the direction of his gaze, she was terrified to see a ship's boat approaching from up-stream, in which, she felt assured, there could be only members of the *Kincaid's* missing crew—only heartless ruffians and enemies.

16

In the Darkness of the Night

WHEN Tarzan of the Apes realized that he was in the grip of the great jaws of a crocodile he did not, as an ordinary man might have done, give up all hope and resign himself to his fate.

Instead, he filled his lungs with air before the huge rep-tile dragged him beneath the surface, and then, with all the might of his great muscles, fought bitterly for freedom. But out of his native element the ape-man was too greatly handi-capped to do more than excite the monster to greater speed as it dragged its prey swiftly through the water.

Tarzan's lungs were bursting for a breath of pure fresh air. He knew that he could survive but a moment more, and in the last paroxysm of his suffering he did what he could to avenge his own death.

His body trailed out beside the slimy carcass of his captor, and into the tough armour the ape-man attempted to plunge his stone knife as he was borne to the creature's horrid den.

His efforts but served to accelerate the speed of the crocodile, and just as the ape-man realized that he had reached the limit of his endurance he felt his body dragged to a muddy bed and his nostrils rise above the water's surface. All about him was the blackness of the pit—the silence of the grave.

For a moment Tarzan of the Apes lay gasping for breath upon the slimy, evil-smelling bed to which the animal had borne him. Close at his side he could feel the cold, hard plates of the creature's coat rising and falling as though with spasmodic efforts to breathe.

For several minutes the two lay thus, and then a sudden convulsion of the giant carcass at the man's side, a tremor, and a stiffening brought Tarzan to his knees beside the crocodile. To his utter amazement he found that the beast was dead. The slim knife had found a vulnerable spot in the scaly armour.

Staggering to his feet, the ape-man groped about the reeking, oozy den. He found that he was imprisoned in a subterranean chamber amply large enough to have accommodated a dozen or more of the huge animal such as the one that had dragged him thither.

He realized that he was in the creature's hidden nest far under the bank of the stream, and that doubtless the only means of ingress or egress lay through the submerged opening through which the crocodile had brought him.

He first thought, of course, was of escape, but that he could make his way to the surface of the river beyond and then to the shore seemed highly improbable. There might be turns and windings in the neck of the passage, or, most to be feared, he might meet another of the slimy imhabitants of the retreat upon his journey outward.

Even should he reach the river in safety, there was still the danger of his being again attacked before he could effect a safe landing. Still there was no alternative, and, filling his lungs with the close and reeking air of the chamber, Tarzan of the Apes dived into the dark and watery hole which he could not see but had felt out and found with his feet and legs.

The leg which had been held within the jaws of the crocodile was badly lacerated, but the bone had not been broken, nor were the muscles or tendons sufficiently injured to render it useless. It gave him excruciating pain, that was all.

But Tarzan of the Apes was accustomed to pain, and gave it no further thought when he found that the use of his legs was not greatly impaired by the sharp teeth of the monster.

Rapidly he crawled and swam through the passage which inclined downward and finally upward to open at last into the river bottom but a few feet from the shore line. As the ape-man reached the surface he saw the heads of two great crocodiles but a short distance from him. They were making rapidly in his direction, and with a superhuman effort the man struck out for the overhanging branches of a near-by tree.

Nor was he a moment too soon, for scarcely had he drawn himself to the safety of the limb than two gaping mouths snapped venomously below him. For a few minutes Tarzan rested in the tree that had proved the means of his salvation. His eyes scanned the river as far down-stream as the tortuous channel would permit, but there was no sign of the Russian or his dugout.

When he had rested and bound up his wounded leg he started on in pursuit of the drifting canoe. He found himself upon the opposite side of the river to that at which he had entered the stream, but as his quarry was upon the bosom of the water it made little difference to the ape-man upon which side he took up the pursuit.

To his intense chagrin he soon found that his leg was more badly injured than he had thought, and that its condition seriously impeded his progress. It was only with the greatest difficulty that he could proceed faster than a walk upon the ground, and in the trees he discovered that it not only impeded his progress, but rendered travelling distinctly dangerous.

From the old negress, Tambudza, Tarzan had gathered a suggestion that now filled his mind with doubts and misgivings. When the old woman had told him of the child's death she had also added that the white woman, though grief-stricken, had confided to her that the baby was not hers.

Tarzan could see no reason for believing that Jane could have found it advisable to deny her identity or that of the child; the only explanation that he could put upon the matter was that, after all, the white woman who had accompanied his son and the Swede into the jungle fastness of the interior had not been Jane at all.

The more he gave thought to the problem, the more

firmly convinced he became that his son was dead and his wife still safe in London, and in ignorance of the terrible fate that had overtaken her first-born.

After all, then, his interpretation of Rokoff's sinister taunt had been erroneous, and he had been bearing the burden of a double apprehension needlessly—at least so thought the ape-man. From this belief he garnered some slight surcease from the numbing grief that the death of his little son had thrust upon him.

And such a death! Even the savage beast that was the real Tarzan, inured to the sufferings and horrors of the grim jungle, shuddered as he contemplated the hideous fate that had overtaken the innocent child.

As he made his way painfully towards the coast, he let his mind dwell so constantly upon the frightful crimes which the Russian had perpetrated against his loved ones that the great scar upon his forehead stood out almost continuously in the vivid scarlet that marked the man's most relentless and bestial moods of rage. At times he startled even himself and sent the lesser creatures of the wild jungle scampering to their hiding places as involuntary roars and growls rumbled from his throat.

Could he but lay his hand upon the Russian!

Twice upon the way to the coast bellicose natives ran threateningly from their villages to bar his further progress, but when the awful cry of the bull-ape thundered upon their affrighted ears, and the great white giant charged bellowing upon them, they had turned and fled into the bush, nor ventured thence until he had safely passed.

Though his progress seemed tantalizingly slow to the ape-man whose idea of speed had been gained by such standards as the lesser apes attain, he made, as a matter of fact, almost as rapid progress as the drifitng canoe that bore Rokoff on ahead of him, so that he came to the bay and within sight of the ocean just after darkness had fallen upon the same day that Jane Clayton and the Russian ended their flights from the interior.

The darkness lowered so heavily upon the black river and the encircling jungle that Tarzan, even with eyes accustomed to much use after dark, could make out nothing a few yards from him. His idea was to search the shore that night for signs of the Russian and the woman who he was certain must have preceded Rokoff down the Ugambi. That the *Kincaid* or other ship lay at anchor but a hundred yards from him he did not dream, for no light showed on board the steamer.

Even as he commenced his search his attention was sud-

denly attracted by a noise that he had not at first perceived
—the stealthy dip of paddles in the water some distance
from the shore, and about opposite the point at which he
stood. Motionless as a statue he stood listening to the faint
sound.

Presently it ceased, to be followed by a shuffling noise
that the ape-man's trained ears could interpret as resulting
from but a single cause—the scraping of leather-shod feet
upon the rounds of a ship's monkey-ladder, And yet, as far
as he could see, there was no ship there—nor might there
be one within a thousand miles.

As he stood thus, peering out into the darkness of the cloud-
enshrouded night, there came to him from across the water,
like a slap in the face, so sudden and unexpected was it, the
sharp staccato of an exchange of shots and then the scream of
a woman.

Wounded though he was, and with the memory of his
recent horrible experience still strong upon him, Tarzan of
the Apes did not hesitate as the notes of that frightened cry
rose shrill and piercing upon the still night air. With a
bound he cleared the intervening bush—there was a splash
as the water closed about him—and then, with powerful
strokes, he swam out into the impenetrable night with no
guide save the memory of an illusive cry, and for company
the hideous denizens of an equatorial river.

The boat that had attracted Jane's attention as she stood
guard upon the deck of the *Kincaid* had been perceived by
Rokoff upon one bank and Mugambi and the horde upon
the other. The cries of the Russian had brought the dugout
first to him, and then, after a conference, it had been turned
toward the *Kincaid*, but before ever it covered half the distance between the shore and the steamer a rifle had spoken
from the latter's deck and one of the sailors in the bow of
the canoe had crumpled and fallen into the water.

After that they went more slowly, and presently, when
Jane's rifle had found another member of the party, the canoe
withdrew to the shore, where it lay as long as daylight lasted.

The savage, snarling pack upon the opposite shore had
been directed in their pursuit by the black warrior, Mugambi,
chief of the Wagambi. Only he knew which might be foe
and which friend of their lost master.

Could they have reached either the canoe or the *Kincaid*
they would have made short work of any whom they found
there, but the gulf of black water intervening shut them off
from farther advance as effectually as though it had been the
broad ocean that separated them from their prey.

Mugambi knew something of the occurrences which had led up to the landing of Tarzan upon Jungle Island and the pursuit of the whites up the Ugambi. He knew that his savage master sought his wife and child who had been stolen by the wicked white man whom they had followed far into the interior and now back to the sea.

He believed also that this same man had killed the great white giant whom he had come to respect and love as he had never loved the greatest chiefs of his own people. And so in the wild breast of Mugambi burned an iron resolve to win to the side of the wicked one and wreak vengeance upon him for the murder of the ape-man.

But when he saw the canoe come down the river and take in Rokoff, when he saw it make for the *Kincaid*, he realized that only by possessing himself of a canoe could he hope to transport the beasts of the pack within striking distance of the enemy.

So it happened that even before Jane Clayton fired the first shot into Rokoff's canoe the beasts of Tarzan had disappeared into the jungle.

After the Russian and his party, which consisted of Paulvitch and the several men he had left upon the *Kincaid* to attend to the matter of coaling, had retreated before her fire, Jane realized that it would be but a temporary respite from their attentions which she had gained, and with the conviction came a determination to make a bold and final stroke for freedom from the menacing threat of Rokoff's evil purpose.

With this idea in view she opened negotiations with the two sailors she had imprisoned in the forecastle, and having forced their consent to her plans, upon pain of death should they attempt disloyalty, she released them just as darkness closed about the ship.

With ready revolver to compel obedience, she let them up one by one, searching them carefully for concealed weapons as they stood with hands elevated above their heads. Once satisfied that they were unarmed, she set them to work cutting the cable which held the *Kincaid* to her anchorage, for her bold plan was nothing less than to set the steamer adrift and float with her out into the open sea, there to trust to the mercy of the elements, which she was confident would be no more merciless than Nikolas Rokoff should he again capture her.

There was, too, the chance that the *Kincaid* might be sighted by some passing ship, and as she was well stocked with provisions and water—the men had assured her of this fact—and as the season of storm was well over, she had every reason to hope for the eventual success of her plan.

The night was deeply overcast, heavy clouds riding low above the jungle and the water—only to the west, where the broad ocean spread beyond the river's mouth, was there a suggestion of lessening gloom.

It was a perfect night for the purposes of the work in hand.

Her enemies could not see the activity aboard the ship nor mark her course as the swift current bore her outward into the ocean. Before daylight broke the ebb-tide would have carried the *Kincaid* well into the Benguela current which flows northward along the coast of Africa, and, as a south wind was prevailing, Jane hoped to be out of sight of the mouth of the Ugambi before Rokoff could become aware of the departure of the steamer.

Standing over the labouring seamen, the young woman breathed a sigh of relief as the last strand of the cable parted and she knew that the vessel was on its way out of the maw of the savage Ugambi.

With her two prisoners still beneath the coercing influence of her rifle, she ordered them upon deck with the intention of again imprisoning them in the forecastle; but at length she permitted herself to be influenced by their promises of loyalty and the arguments which they put forth that they could be of service to her, and permitted them to remain above.

For a few minutes the *Kincaid* drifted rapidly with the current, and then, with a grinding jar, she stopped in mid-stream. The ship had run upon a low-lying bar that splits the channel about a quarter of a mile from the sea.

For a moment she hung there, and then, swinging round until her bow pointed toward the shore, she broke adrift once more.

At the same instant, just as Jane Clayton was congratulating herself that the ship was once more free, there fell upon her ears from a point up the river about where the *Kincaid* had been anchored the rattle of musketry and a woman's scream—shrill, piercing, fear-laden.

The sailors heard the shots with certain conviction that they announced the coming of their employer, and as they had no relish for the plan that would consign them to the deck of a drifting derelict, they whispered together a hurried plan to overcome the young woman and hail Rokoff and their companions to their rescue.

It seemed that fate would play into their hands, for with the reports of the guns Jane Clayton's attention had been distracted from her unwilling assistants, and instead of keep-

ing one eye upon them as she had intended doing, she ran
to the bow of the *Kincaid* to peer through the darkness
toward the source of the distrubance upon the river's bosom.

Seeing that she was off her guard, the two sailors crept
stealthily upon her from behind.

The scraping upon the neck of the shoes of one of them
startled the girl to a sudden appreciation of her danger,
but the warning had come too late.

As she turned, both men leaped upon her and bore her to
the deck, and as she went down beneath them she saw,
outlined against the lesser gloom of the ocean, the figure of
another man clamber over the side of the *Kincaid*.

After all her pains her heroic struggle for freedom had
failed. With a stifled sob she gave up the unequal battle.

17

On the Deck of the "Kincaid"

WHEN Mugambi had turned back into the jungle
with the pack he had a definite purpose in view. It
was to obtain a dugout wherewith to transport the
beasts of Tarzan to the side of the *Kincaid*. Nor was he long
in coming upon the object which he sought.

Just at dusk he found a canoe moored to the bank of a
small tributary of the Ugambi at a point where he had felt
certain that he should find one.

Without loss of time he piled his hideous fellows into the
craft and shoved out into the stream. So quickly had they
taken possession of the canoe that the warrior had not
noticed that it was already occupied. The huddled figure
sleeping in the bottom had entirely escaped his observation
in the darkness of the night that had now fallen.

But no sooner were they afloat than a savage growling
from one of the apes directly ahead of him in the dugout
attracted his attention to a shivering and cowering figure that
trembled between him and the great anthropoid. To Mugambi's astonishment he saw that it was a native woman.
With difficulty he kept the ape from her throat, and after a
time succeeded in quelling her fears.

It seemed that she had been fleeing from marriage with an old man she loathed and had taken refuge for the night in the canoe she had found upon the river's edge.

Mugambi did not wish her presence, but there she was, and rather than lose time by returning her to the shore the black permitted her to remain on board the canoe.

As quickly as his awkward companions could paddle the dugout down-stream toward the Ugambi and the *Kincaid* they moved through the darkness. It was with difficulty that Mugambi could make out the shadowy form of the steamer, but as he had it between himself and the ocean it was much more apparent than to one upon either shore of the river.

As he approached it he was amazed to note that it seemed to be receding from him, and finally he was convinced that the vessel was moving down-stream. Just as he was about to urge his creatures to renewed efforts to overtake the steamer the outline of another canoe burst suddenly into view not three yards from the bow of his own craft.

At the same instant the occupants of the stranger discovered the proximity of Mugambi's horde, but they did not at first recognize the nature of the fearful crew. A man in the bow of the oncoming boat challenged them just as the two dugouts were about to touch.

For answer came the menacing growl of a panther, and the fellow found himself gazing into the flaming eyes of Sheeta, who had raised himself with his forepaws upon the bow of the boat, ready to leap in upon the occupants of the other craft.

Instantly Rokoff realized the peril that confronted him and his fellows. He gave a quick command to fire upon the occupants of the other canoe, and it was this volley and the scream of the terrified native woman in the canoe with Mugambi that both Tarzan and Jane had heard.

Before the slower and less skilled paddlers in Mugambi's canoe could press their advantage and effect a boarding of the enemy the latter had turned swiftly down-stream and were paddling for their lives in the direction of the *Kincaid*, which was now visible to them.

The vessel after striking upon the bar had swung loose again into a slow-moving eddy, which returns up-stream close to the southern shore of the Ugambi only to circle out once more and join the downward flow a hundred yards or so farther up. Thus the *Kincaid* was returning Jane Clayton directly into the hands of her enemies.

It so happened that as Tarzan sprang into the river the vessel was not visible to him, and as he swam out into the night he had no idea that a ship drifted so close at hand. He was guided by the sounds which he could hear coming from the two canoes.

As he swam he had vivid recollections of the last occasion upon which he had swum in the waters of the Ugambi, and with them a sudden shudder shook the frame of the giant.

But, though he twice felt something brush his legs from the slimy depths below him, nothing seized him, and of a sudden he quite forgot about crocodiles in the astonishment of seeing a dark mass loom suddenly before him where he had still expected to find the open river.

So close was it that a few strokes brought him up to the thing, when to his amazement his outstretched hand came in contact with a ship's side.

As the agile ape-man clambered over the vessel's rail there came to his sensitive ears the sound of a struggle at the opposite side of the deck.

Noiselessly he sped across the intervening space.

The moon had risen now, and, though the sky was still banked with clouds, a lesser darkness enveloped the scene than that which had blotted out all sight earlier in the night. His keen eyes, therefore, saw the figures of two men grappling with a woman.

That it was the woman who had accompanied Anderssen toward the interior he did not know, though he suspected as much, as he was now quite certain that this was the deck of the *Kincaid* upon which chance had led him.

But he wasted little time in idle speculation. There was a woman in danger of harm from two ruffians, which was enough excuse for the ape-man to project his giant thews into the conflict without further investigation.

The first that either of the sailors knew that there was a new force at work upon the ship was the falling of a mighty hand upon a shoulder of each. As if they had been in the grip of a fly-wheel, they were jerked suddenly from their prey.

"What means this?" asked a low voice in their ears.

They were given no time to reply, however, for at the sound of that voice the young woman had sprung to her feet and with a little cry of joy leaped toward their assailant.

"Tarzan!" she cried.

The ape-man hurled the two sailors across the deck, where they rolled, stunned and terrified, into the scuppers upon the opposite side, and with an exclamation of incredulity gathered the girl into his arms.

Brief, however, were the moments for their greeting.

Scarcely had they recognized one another than the

clouds above them parted to show the figures of a half-dozen men clambering over the side of the *Kincaid* to the steamer's deck.

Foremost among them was the Russian. As the brilliant rays of the equatorial moon lighted the deck, and he realized that the man before him was Lord Greystoke, he screamed hysterical commands to his followers to fire upon the two.

Tarzan pushed Jane behind the cabin near which they had been standing, and with a quick bound started for Rokot. The men behind the Russian, at least two of them, raised their rifles and fired at the charging ape-man; but those behind them were otherwise engaged—for up the monkey-ladder in their rear was thronging a hideous horde.

First came five snarling apes, huge, manlike beasts, with bared fangs and slavering jaws; and after them a giant black warrior, his long spear gleaming in the moonlight.

Behind him again scrambled another creature, and of all the horrid horde it was this they most feared—Sheeta, the panther, with gleaming jaws agape and fiery eyes blazing at them in the mightiness of his hate and of his blood lust.

The shots that had been fired at Tarzan missed him, and he would have been upon Rokoff in another instant had not the great coward dodged backward between his two henchmen, and, screaming in hysterical terror, bolted forward toward the forecastle.

For the moment Tarzan's attention was distracted by the two men before him, so that he could not at the time pursue the Russian. About him the apes and Mugambi were battling with the balance of the Russian's party.

Beneath the terrible ferocity of the beasts the men were soon scampering in all directions—those who still lived to scamper, for the great fangs of the apes of Akut and the tearing talons of Sheeta already had found more than a single victim.

Four, however, escaped and disappeared into the forecastle, where they hoped to barricade themselves against further assault. Here they found Rokoff, and, enraged at his desertion of them in their moment of peril, no less than at the uniformly brutal treatment it had been his wont to accord them, they gloated upon the opportunity now offered them to revenge themselves in part upon their hated employer.

Despite his prayers and grovelling pleas, therefore, they hurled him bodily out upon the deck, delivering him to the mercy of the fearful things from which they had themselves just escaped.

Tarzan saw the man emerge from the forecastle—saw

and recognized his enemy; but another saw him even as soon.

It was Sheeta, and with grinning jaws the mighty beast slunk silently toward the terror-stricken man.

When Rokoff saw what it was that stalked him his shrieks for help filled the air, as with trembling knees he stood, as one paralyzed, before the hideous death that was creeping upon him.

Tarzan took a step toward the Russian, his brain burning with a raging fire of vengeance. At last he had the murderer of his son at his mercy. His was the right to avenge.

Once Jane had stayed his hand that time that he sought to take the law into his own power and mete to Rokoff the death that he had so long merited; but this time none should stay him.

His fingers clenched and unclenched spasmodically as he approached the trembling Russ, beastlike and ominous as a brute of prey.

Presently he saw that Sheeta was about to forestall him, robbing him of the fruits of his great hate.

He called sharply to the panther, and the words, as if they had broken a hideous spell that had held the Russian, galvanized him into sudden action. With a scream he turned and fled toward the bridge.

After him pounced Sheeta the panther, unmindful of his master's warning voice.

Tarzan was about to leap after the two when he felt a light touch upon his arm. Turning, he found Jane at his elbow.

"Do not leave me," she whispered. "I am afraid."

Tarzan glanced behind her.

All about were the hideous apes of Akut. Some, even, were approaching the young woman with bared fangs and menacing guttural warnings.

The ape-man warned them back. He had forgotten for the moment that these were but beasts, unable to differentiate his friends and his foes. Their savage natures were roused by their recent battle with the sailors, and now all flesh outside the pack was meat to them.

Tarzan turned again toward the Russian, chagrined that he should have to forgo the pleasure of personal revenge—unless the man should escape Sheeta. But as he looked he saw that there could be no hope of that. The fellow had retreated to the end of the bridge, where he now stood trembling and wide-eyed, facing the beast that moved slowly toward him.

The panther crawled with belly to the planking, uttering uncanny mouthings. Rokoff stood as though petrified, his eyes protruding from their sockets, his mouth agape, and the cold sweat of terror clammy upon his brow.

Below him, upon the deck, he had seen the great anthropoids, and so had not dared to seek escape in that direction. In fact, even now one of the brutes was leaping to seize the bridge-rail and draw himself up to the Russian's side.

Before him was the panther, silent and crouched.

Rokoff could not move. His knees trembled. His voice broke in inarticulate shrieks. With a last piercing wail he sank to his knees—and then Sheeta sprang.

Full upon the man's breast the tawny body hurtled, tumbling the Russian to his back.

As the great fangs tore at the throat and chest, Jane Clayton turned away in horror; but not so Tarzan of the Apes. A cold smile of satisfaction touched his lips. The scar upon his forehead that had burned scarlet faded to the normal hue of his tanned skin and disappeared.

Rokoff fought furiously but futilely against the growling, rending fate that had overtaken him. For all his countless crimes he was punished in the brief moment of the hideous death that claimed him at the last.

After his struggles ceased Tarzan approached, at Jane's suggestion, to wrest the body from the panther and give what remained of it decent human burial; but the great cat rose snarling above its kill, threatening even the master it loved in its savage way, so that rather than kill his friend of the jungle, Tarzan was forced to relinquish his intentions.

All that night Sheeta, the panther, crouched upon the grisly thing that had been Nikolas Rokoff. The bridge of the *Kincaid* was slippery with blood. Beneath the brilliant tropic moon the great beast feasted until, when the sun rose the following morning, there remained of Tarzan's great enemy only gnawed and broken bones.

Of the Russian's party, all were accounted for except Paulvitch. Four were prisoners in the *Kincaid's* forecastle. The rest were dead.

With these men Tarzan got up steam upon the vessel, and with the knowledge of the mate, who happened to be one of those surviving, he planned to set out in quest of Jungle Island; but as the morning dawned there came with it a heavy gale from the west which raised a sea into which the mate of the *Kincaid* dared not venture. All that day the ship lay within the shelter of the mouth of the river; for, though night witnessed a lessening of the wind, it was thought safer to wait for daylight before attempting the navigation of the winding channel to the sea.

Upon the deck of the steamer the pack wandered without let or hindrance by day, for they had soon learned through Tarzan and Mugambi that they must harm no one upon the *Kincaid*; but at night they were confined below.

Tarzan's joy had been unbounded when he learned from his wife that the little child who had died in the village of M'ganwazam was not their son. Who the baby could have been, or what had become of their own, they could not imagine, and as both Rokoff and Paulvitch were gone, there was no way of discovering.

There was, however, a certain sense of relief in the knowledge that they might yet hope. Until positive proof of the baby's death reached them there was always that to buoy them up.

It seemed quite evident that their little Jack had not been brought aboard the *Kincaid*. Anderssen would have known of it had such been the case, but he had assured Jane time and time again that the little one he had brought to her cabin the night he aided her to escape was the only one that had been aboard the *Kincaid* since she lay at Dover.

18

Paulvitch Plots Revenge

A S Jane and Tarzan stood upon the vessel's deck recounting to one another the details of the various adventures through which each had passed since they had parted in their London home, there glared at them from beneath scowling brows a hidden watcher upon the shore.

Through the man's brain passed plan after plan whereby he might thwart the escape of the Englishman and his wife, for so long as the vital spark remained within the vindictive brain of Alexander Paulvitch none who had aroused the enmity of the Russian might be entirely safe.

Plan after plan he formed only to discard each either as impracticable, or unworthy the vengeance his wrongs demanded. So warped by faulty reasoning was the criminal mind of Rokoff's lieutenant that he could not grasp the real truth of that which lay between himself and the ape-man and see that always the fault had been, not with the English lord, but with himself and his confederate.

And at the rejection of each new scheme Paulvitch arrived always at the same conclusion—that he could accomplish naught while half the breadth of the Ugambi separated him from the object of his hatred.

But how was he to span the crocodile-infested waters? There was no canoe nearer than the Mosula village, and Paulvitch was none too sure that the *Kincaid* would still be at anchor in the river when he returned should he take the time to traverse the jungle to the distant village and return with a canoe. Yet there was no other way, and so, convinced that thus alone might he hope to reach his prey, Paulvitch, with a parting scowl at the two figures upon the *Kincaid*'s deck, turned away from the river.

Hastening through the dense jungle, his mind centred upon his one fetich—revenge—the Russian forgot even his terror of the savage world through which he moved.

Baffled and beaten at every turn of Fortune's wheel, reacted upon time after time by his own malign plotting, the principal victim of his own criminality, Paulvitch was yet so blind as to imagine that his greatest happiness lay in a continuation of the plottings and schemings which had ever brought him and Rokoff to disaster, and the latter finally to a hideous death.

As the Russian stumbled on through the jungle toward the Mosula village there presently crystallized within his brain a plan which seemed more feasible than any that he had as yet considered.

He would come by night to the side of the *Kincaid*, and, once aboard, would search out the members of the ship's original crew who had survived the terrors of this frightful expedition, and enlist them in an attempt to wrest the vessel from Tarzan and his beasts.

In the cabin were arms and ammunition, and hidden in a secret receptacle in the cabin table was one of those infernal machines, the construction of which had occupied much of Paulvitch's spare time when he had stood high in the confidence of the Nihilists of his native land.

That was before he had sold them out for immunity and gold to the police of Petrograd. Paulvitch winced as he recalled the denunciation of him that had fallen from the lips of one of his former comrades ere the poor devil expiated his political sins at the end of a hempen rope.

But the infernal machine was the thing to think of now. He could do much with that if he could but get his hands upon it. Within the little hardwood case hidden in the cabin

table rested sufficient potential destructiveness to wipe out
in the fraction of a second every enemy aboard the *Kincaid*.

Paulvitch licked his lips in anticipatory joy, and urged
his tired legs to greater speed that he might not be too late
to the ship's anchorage to carry out his designs.

All depended, of course, upon when the *Kincaid* departed. The Russian realized that nothing could be accomplished beneath the light of day. Darkness must shroud
his approach to the ship's side, for should he be sighted by
Tarzan or Lady Greystoke he would have no chance to
board the vessel.

The gale that was blowing was, he believed, the cause of
the delay in getting the *Kincaid* under way, and if it continued to blow until night then the chances were all in his
favour, for he knew that there was little likelihood of the
ape-man attempting to navigate the tortuous channel of
the Ugambi while darkness lay upon the surface of the water,
hiding the many bars and the numerous small islands which
are scattered over the expanse of the river's mouth.

It was well after noon when Paulvitch came to the Mosula village upon the bank of the tributary of the Ugambi.
Here he was received with suspicion and unfriendliness by
the native chief, who, like all those who came in contact
with Rokoff or Paulvitch, had suffered in some manner from
the greed, the cruelty, or the lust of the two Muscovites.

When Paulvitch demanded the use of a canoe the chief
grumbled a surly refusal and ordered the white man from
the village. Surrounded by angry, muttering warriors who
seemed to be but waiting some slight pretext to transfix him
with their menacing spears the Russian could do naught else
than withdraw.

A dozen fighting men led him to the edge of the clearing,
leaving him with a warning never to show himself again in
the vicinity of their village.

Stifling his anger, Paulvitch slunk into the jungle; but
once beyond the sight of the warriors he paused and listened
intently. He could hear the voices of his escort as the men
returned to the village, and when he was sure that they were
not following him he wormed his way through the bushes to
the edge of the river, still determined some way to obtain
a canoe.

Life itself depended upon his reaching the *Kincaid* and
enlisting the survivors of the ship's crew in his service,
for to be abandoned here amidst the dangers of the African
jungle where he had won the enmity of the natives was, he
well knew, partically equivalent to a sentence of death.

A desire for revenge acted as an almost equally powerful

incentive to spur him into the face of danger to accomplish his design, so that it was a desperate man that lay hidden in the foliage beside the little river searching with eager eyes for some sign of a small canoe which might be easily handled by a single paddle.

Nor had the Russian long to wait before one of the awkward little skiffs which the Mosula fashion came in sight upon the bosom of the river. A youth was paddling lazily out into midstream from a point beside the village. When he reached the channel he allowed the sluggish current to carry him slowly along while he lolled indolently in the bottom of his crude canoe.

All ignorant of the unseen enemy upon the river's bank the lad floated slowly down the stream while Paulvitch followed along the jungle path a few yards behind him.

A mile below the village the black boy dipped his paddle into the water and forced his skiff toward the bank. Paulvitch, elated by the chance which had drawn the youth to the same side of the river as that along which he followed rather than to the opposite side where he would have been beyond the stalker's reach, hid in the brush close beside the point at which it was evident the skiff would touch the bank of the slow-moving stream, which seemed jealous of each fleeting instant which drew it nearer to the broad and muddy Ugambi where it must for ever lose its identity in the larger stream that would presently cast its waters into the great ocean.

Equally indolent were the motions of the Mosula youth as he drew his skiff beneath an overhanging limb of a great tree that leaned down to implant a farewell kiss upon the bosom of the departing water, caressing with green fronds the soft breast of its languorous love.

And, snake-like, amidst the concealing foliage lay the malevolent Russ. Cruel, shifty eyes gloated upon the outlines of the coveted canoe, and measured the stature of its owner, while the crafty brain weighed the chances of the white man should physical encounter with the black become necessary.

Only direst necessity could drive Alexander Paulvitch to personal conflict; but it was indeed dire necessity which goaded him on to action now.

There was time, just time enough, to reach the *Kincaid* by nightfall. Would the black fool never quit his skiff? Paulvitch squirmed and fidgeted. The lad yawned and stretched. With exasperating deliberateness he examined the arrows in his quiver, tested his bow, and looked to the edge upon the hunting-knife in his loin-cloth.

Again he stretched and yawned, glanced up at the river-bank, shrugged his shoulders, and lay down in the bottom of his canoe for a little nap before he plunged into the jungle after the prey he had come forth to hunt.

Paulvitch half rose, and with tensed muscles stood glaring down upon his unsuspecting victim. The boy's lids drooped and closed. Presently his breast rose and fell to the deep breaths of slumber. The time had come!

The Russian crept stealthily nearer. A branch rustled beneath his weight and the lad stirred in his sleep. Paulvitch drew his revolver and levelled it upon the black. For a moment he remained in rigid quiet, and then again the youth relapsed into undisturbed slumber.

The white man crept closer. He could not chance a shot until there was no risk of missing. Presently he leaned close above the Mosula. The cold steel of the revolver in his hand insinuated itself nearer and nearer to the breast of the unconsious lad. Now it stopped but a few inches above the strongly beating heart.

But the pressure of a finger lay between the harmless boy and eternity. The soft bloom of youth still lay upon the brown cheek, a smile half parted the beardless lips. Did any qualm of conscience point its disquieting finger of reproach at the murderer?

To all such was Alexander Paulvitch immune. A sneer curled his bearded lip as his forefinger closed upon the trigger of his revolver. There was a loud report. A little hole appeared above the heart of the sleeping boy, a little hole about which lay a blackened rim of powder-burned flesh.

The youthful body half rose to a sitting posture. The smiling lips tensed to the nervous shock of a momentary agony which the conscious mind never apprehended, and then the dead sank limply back into that deepest of slumbers from which there is no awakening.

The killer dropped quickly into the skiff beside the killed. Ruthless hands seized the dead boy heartlessly and raised him to the low gunwale. A little shove, a splash, some widening ripples broken by the sudden surge of a dark, hidden body from the slimy depths, and the coveted canoe was in the sole possession of the white man—more savage than the youth whose life he had taken.

Casting off the tie rope and seizing the paddle, Paulvitch bent feverishly to the task of driving the skiff downward toward the Ugambi at top speed.

Night had fallen when the prow of the bloodstained craft shot out into the current of the larger stream. Constantly the Russian strained his eyes into the increasing darkness ahead

in vain endeavour to pierce the black shadows which lay
between him and the anchorage of the *Kincaid*.

Was the ship still riding there upon the waters of the
Ugambi, or had the ape-man at last persuaded himself of the
safety of venturing forth into the abating storm? As Paulvitch forged ahead with the current he asked himself these
questions, and many more beside, not the least disquieting
of which were those which related to his future should it
chance that the *Kincaid* had already steamed away, leaving
him to the merciless horrors of the savage wilderness.

In the darkness it seemed to the paddler that he was
fairly flying over the water, and he had become convinced
that the ship had left her moorings and that he had already
passed the spot at which she had lain earlier in the day, when
there appeared before him beyond a projecting point which
he had but just rounded the flickering light from a ship's
lantern.

Alexander Paulvitch could scarce restrain an exclamation
of triumph. The *Kincaid* had not departed! Life and vengeance were not to elude him after all.

He stopped paddling the moment that he descried the
gleaming beacon of hope ahead of him. Silently he drifted
down the muddy waters of the Ugambi, occasionally dipping
his paddle's blade gently into the current that he might guide
his primitive craft to the vessel's side.

As he approached more closely the dark bulk of a ship
loomed before him out of the blackness of the night. No
sound came from the vessel's deck. Paulvitch drifted, unseen,
close to the *Kincaid*'s side. Only the momentary scraping of
his canoe's nose against the ship's planking broke the silence
of the night.

Trembling with nervous excitement, the Russian remained
motionless for several minutes; but there was no sound from
the great bulk above him to indicate that his coming had
been noted.

Stealthily he worked his craft forward until the stays of
the bowsprit were directly above him. He could just reach
them. To make his canoe fast there was the work of but a
minute or two, and then the man raised himself quietly aloft.

A moment later he dropped softly to the deck. Thoughts
of the hideous pack which tenanted the ship induced cold
tremors along the spine of the cowardly prowler; but life
itself depended upon the success of his venture, and so he
was enabled to steel himself to the frightful chances which
lay before him.

No sound or sign of watch appeared upon the ship's deck.
Paulvitch crept stealthily toward the forecastle. All was

silence. The hatch was raised, and as the man peered downward he saw one of the *Kincaid*'s crew reading by the light of the smoky lantern depending from the ceiling of the crew's quarters.

Paulvitch knew the man well, a surly cut-throat upon whom he figured strongly in the carrying out of the plan which he had conceived. Gently the Russ lowered himself through the aperture to the rounds of the ladder which led into the forecastle.

He kept his eyes turned upon the reading man, ready to warn him to silence the moment that the fellow discovered him; but so deeply immersed was the sailor in the magazine that the Russian came, unobserved, to the forecastle floor.

There he turned and whispered the reader's name. The man raised his eyes from the magazine—eyes that went wide for a moment as they fell upon the familiar countenance of Rokoff's lieutenant, only to narrow instantly in a scowl of disapproval.

"The devil!" he ejaculated. "Where did you come from? We all thought you were done for and gone where you ought to have gone a long time ago. His lordship will be mighty pleased to see you."

Paulvitch crossed to the sailor's side. A friendly smile lay on the Russian's lips, and his right hand was extended in greeting, as though the other might have been a dear and long lost friend. The sailor ignored the proffered hand, nor did he return the other's smile.

"I've come to help you," explained Paulvitch. "I'm going to help you get rid of the Englishman and his beasts—then there will be no danger from the law when we get back to civilization. We can sneak in on them while they sleep— that is Greystoke, his wife, and that black scoundrel, Mugambi. Afterward it will be a simple matter to clean up the beasts. Where are they?"

"They're below," replied the sailor; "but just let me tell you something, Paulvitch. You haven't got no more show to turn us men against the Englishman than nothing. We had all we wanted of you and that other beast. He's dead, an' if I don't miss my guess a whole lot you'll be dead too before long. You two treated us like dogs, and if you think we got any love for you you better forget it."

"You mean to say that you're going to turn against me?" demanded Paulvitch.

The other nodded, and then after a momentary pause, during which an idea seemed to have occurred to him, he spoke again.

"Unless," he said, "you can make it worth my while to let you go before the Englishman finds you here."

"You wouldn't turn me away in the jungle, would you?" asked Paulvitch. "Why, I'd die there in a week."

"You'd have a chance there," replied the sailor. "Here, you wouldn't have no chance. Why, if I woke up my maties here they'd probably cut your heart out of you before the Englishman got a chance at you at all. It's mighty lucky for you that I'm the one to be awake now and not none of the others."

"You're crazy," cried Paulvitch. "Don't you know that the Englishman will have you all hanged when he gets you back where the law can get hold of you?"

"No, he won't do nothing of the kind," replied the sailor. "He's told us as much, for he says that there wasn't nobody to blame but you and Rokoff—the rest of us was just tools. See?"

For half an hour the Russian pleaded or threatened as the mood seized him. Sometimes he was upon the verge of tears, and again he was promising his listener either fabulous rewards or condign punishment; but the other was obdurate.

He made it plain to the Russian that there were but two plans open to him—either he must consent to being turned over immediately to Lord Greystoke, or he must pay to the sailor, as a price for permission to quit the *Kincaid* unmolested, every cent of money and article of value upon his person and in his cabin.

"And you'll have to make up your mind mighty quick," growled the man, "for I want to turn in. Come now, choose —his lordship or the jungle?"

"You'll be sorry for this," grumbled the Russian.

"Shut up," admonished the sailor. "If you get funny I may change my mind, and keep you here after all."

Now Paulvitch had no intention of permitting himself to fall into the hands of Tarzan of the Apes if he could possibly avoid it, and while the terrors of the jungle appalled him they were, to his mind, infinitely preferable to the certain death which he knew he merited and for which he might look at the hands of the ape-man.

"Is anyone sleeping in my cabin?" he asked.

The sailor shook his head. "No," he said; "Lord and Lady Greystoke have the captain's cabin. The mate is in his own, and there ain't no one in yours."

"I'll go and get my valuables for you," said Paulvitch.

"I'll go with you to see that you don't try any funny business," said the sailor, and he followed the Russian up the ladder to the deck.

At the cabin entrance the sailor halted to watch, permitting Paulvitch to go alone to his cabin. Here he gathered together his few belongings that were to buy him the uncertain safety of escape, and as he stood for a moment beside the little table on which he had piled them he searched his brain for some feasible plan either to ensure his safety or to bring revenge upon his enemies.

And presently as he thought there recurred to his memory the little black box which lay hidden in a secret receptacle beneath a false top upon the table where his hand rested.

The Russian's face lighted to a sinister gleam of malevolent satisfaction as he stooped and felt beneath the table top. A moment later he withdrew from its hiding-place the thing he sought. He had lighted the lantern swinging from the beams overhead that he might see to collect his belongings, and now he held the black box well in the rays of the lamplight, while he fingered at the clasp that fastened its lid.

The lifted cover revealed two compartments within the box. In one was a mechanism which resembled the works of a small clock. There also was a little battery of two dry cells. A wire ran from the clockwork to one of the poles of the battery, and from the other pole through the partition into the other compartment, a second wire returning directly to the clockwork.

Whatever lay within the second compartment was not visible, for a cover lay over it and appeared to be sealed in place by asphaltum. In the bottom of the box, beside the clockwork, lay a key, and this Paulvitch now withdrew and fitted to the winding stem.

Gently he turned the key, muffling the noise of the winding operation by throwing a couple of articles of clothing over the box. All the time he listened intently for any sound which might indicate that the sailor or another were approaching his cabin; but none came to interrupt his work.

When the winding was completed the Russian set a pointer upon a small dial at the side of the clockwork, then he replaced the cover upon the black box, and returned the entire machine to its hiding-place in the table.

A sinister smile curled the man's bearded lips as he gathered up his valuables, blew out the lamp, and stepped from his cabin to the side of the waiting sailor.

"Here are my things," said the Russian; "now let me go."

"I'll first take a look in your pockets," replied the sailor. "You might have overlooked some trifling thing that won't be of no use to you in the jungle, but that'll come in mighty handy to a poor sailorman in London. Ah! just as I

feared," he ejaculated an instant later as he withdrew a roll
of bank-notes from Paulvitch's inside coat pocket.

The Russian scowled, muttering an imprecation; but nothing could be gained by argument, and so he did his best
to reconcile himself to his loss in the knowledge that the
sailor would never reach London to enjoy the fruits of his
thievery.

It was with difficulty that Paulvitch restrained a consum-
ing desire to taunt the man with a suggestion of the fate that
would presently overtake him and the other members of the
Kincaid's company; but fearing to arouse the fellow's suspicions, he crossed the deck and lowered himself in silence
into his canoe.

A minute or two later he was paddling toward the shore
to be swallowed up in the darkness of the jungle night, and
the terrors of a hideous existence from which, could he have
had even a slight foreknowledge of what awaited him in the
long years to come, he would have fled to the certain death
of the open sea rather than endure it.

The sailor, having made sure that Paulvitch had departed,
returned to the forecastle, where he hid away his booty
and turned into his bunk, while in the cabin that had belonged to the Russian there ticked on and on through the
silences of the night the little mechanism in the small black
box which held for the unconscious sleepers upon the ill-
starred *Kincaid* the coming vengance of the thwarted Russian.

19

The Last of the "Kincaid"

SHORTLY after the break of day Tarzan was on deck
noting the condition of the weather. The wind had
abated. The sky was cloudless. Every condition seemed
ideal for the commencement of the return voyage to
Jungle Island, where the beasts were to be left. And then—
home!

The ape-man aroused the mate and gave instructions that
the *Kincaid* sail at the earliest possible moment. The remaining members of the crew, safe in Lord Greystoke's

assurance that they would not be prosecuted for their share in the villainies of the two Russians, hastened with cheerful alacrity to their several duties.

The beasts, liberated from the confinement of the hold, wandered about the deck, not a little to the discomfiture of the crew in whose minds there remained a still vivid picture of the savagery of the beasts in conflict with those who had gone to their deaths beneath the fangs and talons which even now seemed itching for the soft flesh of further prey.

Beneath the watchful eyes of Tarzan and Mugambi, however, Sheeta and the apes of Akut curbed their desires, so that the men worked about the deck amongst them in far greater security than they imagined.

At last the *Kincaid* slipped down the Ugambi and ran out upon the shimmering waters of the Atlantic. Tarzan and Jane Clayton watched the verdure-clad shore-line receding in the ship's wake, and for once the ape-man left his native soil without one single pang of regret.

No ship that sailed the seven seas could have borne him away from Africa to resume his search for his lost boy with half the speed that the Englishman would have desired, and the slow-moving *Kincaid* seemed scarce to move at all to the impatient mind of the bereaved father.

Yet the vessel made progress even when she seemed to be standing still, and presently the low hills of Jungle Island became distinctly visible upon the western horizon ahead.

In the cabin of Alexander Paulvitch the thing within the black box ticked, ticked, ticked, with apparently unending monotony; but yet, second by second, a little arm which protruded from the periphery of one of its wheels came nearer and nearer to another little arm which projected from the hand which Paulvitch had set at a certain point upon the dial beside the clockwork. When those two arms touched one another the ticking of the mechanism would cease—for ever.

Jane and Tarzan stood upon the bridge looking out toward Jungle Island. The men were forward, also watching the land grow upward out of the ocean. The beasts had sought the shade of the galley, where they were curled up in sleep. All was quiet and peace upon the ship, and upon the waters.

Suddenly, without warning, the cabin roof shot up into the air, a cloud of dense smoke puffed far above the *Kincaid*, there was a terrific explosion which shook the vessel from stem to stern.

Instantly pandemonium broke loose upon the deck. The apes of Akut, terrified by the sound, ran hither and thither, snarling and growling. Sheeta leaped here and there, screaming out his startled terror in hideous cries that sent the ice of fear straight to the hearts of the *Kincaid's* crew.

Mugambi, too, was trembling. Only Tarzan of the Apes and his wife retained their composure. Scarce had the debris settled than the ape-man was among the beasts, quieting their fears, talking to them in low, pacific tones, stroking their shaggy bodies, and assuring them, as only he could, that the immediate danger was over.

An examination of the wreckage showed that their greatest danger, now, lay in fire, for the flames were licking hungrily at the splintered wood of the wrecked cabin, and had already found a foothold upon the lower deck through a great jagged hole which the explosion had opened.

By a miracle no member of the ship's company had been injured by the blast, the origin of which remained for ever a total mystery to all but one—the sailor who knew that Paulvitch had been aboard the *Kincaid* and in his cabin the previous night. He guessed the truth; but discretion sealed his lips. It would, doubtless, fare none too well for the man who had permitted the arch enemy of them all aboard the ship in the watches of the night, where later he might set an infernal machine to blow them all to kingdom-come. No, the man decided that he would keep this knowledge to himself.

As the flames gained headway it became apparent to Tarzan, that whatever had caused the explosion had scattered some highly inflammable substance upon the surrounding woodwork, for the water which they poured in from the pump seemed rather to spread than to extinguish the blaze.

Fifteen minutes after the explosion great, black clouds of smoke were rising from the hold of the doomed vessel. The flames had reached the engine-room, and the ship no longer moved toward the shore. Her fate was as certain as though the waters alreday had closed above her charred and smoking remains.

"It is useless to remain aboard her longer," remarked the ape-man to the mate. "There is no telling but there may be other explosions, and as we cannot hope to save her, the safest thing which we can do is to take to the boats without further loss of time and make land."

Nor was there other alternative. Only the sailors could bring away any belongings, for the fire, which had not yet reached the forecastle, had consumed all in the vicinity of the cabin which the explosion had not destroyed.

Two boats were lowered, and as there was no sea the landing was made with infinite ease. Eager and anxious, the beasts of Tarzan sniffed the familiar air of their native

island as the small boats drew in toward the beach, and
scarce had their keels grated upon the sand than Sheeta and
the apes of Akut were over the bows and racing swiftly toward the jungle.

A half-sad smile curved the lips of the ape-man as he
watched them go.

"Good-bye, my friends," he murmured. "You have been
good and faithful allies, and I shall miss you."

"They will return, will they not, dear?" asked Jane Clayton, at his side.

"They may and they may not," replied the ape-man. "They
have been ill at ease since they were forced to accept so
many human beings into their confidence. Mugambi and I
alone affected them less, for he and I are, at best, but half
human. You, however, and the members of the crew are
far too civilized for my beasts—it is you whom they are
fleeing. Doubtless they feel that they cannot trust themselves
in the close vicinity of so much perfectly good food without the danger that they may help themselves to a mouthful
some time by mistake."

Jane laughed. "I think they are just trying to escape you,"
she retorted. "You are always making them stop something which they see no reason why they should not do.
Like little children they are doubtless delighted at this opportunity to flee from the zone of parental discipline. If
they come back, though, I hope they won't come by night."

"Or come hungry, eh?" laughed Tarzan.

For two hours after landing the little party stood watching the burning ship which they had abandoned. Then there
came faintly to them from across the water the sound of a
second explosion. The *Kincaid* settled rapidly almost immediately thereafter, and sank within a few minutes.

The cause of the second explosion was less a mystery than
that of the first, the mate attributing it to the bursting of
the boilers when the flames had finally reached them; but
what had caused the first explosion was a subject of considerable speculation among the stranded company.

20

Jungle Island Again

THE first consideration of the party was to locate fresh
water and make camp, for all knew that their term of
existence upon Jungle Island might be drawn out to
months, or even years.

Tarzan knew the nearest water, and to this he immediately
led the party. Here the men fell to work to construct shelters and rude furniture while Tarzan went into the jungle
after meat, leaving the faithful Mugambi and the Mosula
woman to guard Jane, whose safety he would never trust
to any member of the *Kincaid's* cut-throat crew.

Lady Greystoke suffered far greater anguish than any
other of the castaways, for the blow to her hopes and her
already cruelly lacerated mother-heart lay not in her own
privations but in the knowledge that she might now never
be able to learn the fate of her first-born or do aught to discover his whereabouts, or ameliorate his condition—a condition which imagination naturally pictured in the most
frightful forms.

For two weeks the party divided the time amongst the
various duties which had been allotted to each. A daylight
watch was maintained from sunrise to sunset upon a bluff
near the camp—a jutting shoulder of rock which overlooked
the sea. Here, ready for instant lighting, was gathered a huge
pile of dry branches, while from a lofty pole which they had
set in the ground there floated an improvised distress signal fashioned from a red undershirt which belonged to the
mate of the *Kincaid*.

But never a speck upon the horizon that might be sail or
smoke rewarded the tired eyes that in their endless, hopeless vigil strained daily out across the vast expanse of ocean.

It was Tarzan who suggested, finally, that they attempt
to construct a vessel that would bear them back to the main-

land. He alone could show them how to fashion rude tools, and when the idea had taken root in the minds of the men they were eager to commence their labours.

But as time went on and the Herculean nature of their task became more and more apparent they fell to grumbling, and to quarrelling among themselves, so that to the other dangers were now added dissension and suspicion.

More than before did Tarzan now fear to leave Jane among the half brutes of the Kincaid's crew; but hunting he must do, for none other could so surely go forth and return with meat as he. Sometimes Mugambi spelled him at the hunting; but the black's spear and arrows were never so sure of results as the rope and knife of the ape-man.

Finally the men shirked their work, going off into the jungle by twos to explore and to hunt. All this time the camp had had no sight of Sheeta, or Akut and the other great apes, though Tarzan had sometimes met them in the jungle as he hunted.

And as matters tended from bad to worse in the camp of the castaways upon the east coast of Jungle Island, another camp came into being upon the north coast.

Here, in a little cove, lay a small schooner, the *Cowrie*, whose decks had but a few days since run red with the blood of her officers and the loyal members of her crew, for the *Cowrie* had fallen upon bad days when it had shipped such men as Gust and Momulla the Maori and that arch-fiend Kai Shang of Fachan.

There were others, too, ten of them all told, the scum of the South Sea ports; but Gust and Momulla and Kai Shang were the brains and cunning of the company. It was they who had instigated the mutiny that they might seize and divide the catch of pearls which constituted the wealth of the *Cowrie*'s cargo.

It was Kai Shang who had murdered the captain as he lay asleep in his berth, and it had been Momulla the Maori who had led the attack upon the officer of the watch.

Gust, after his own peculiar habit, had found means to delegate to the others the actual taking of life. Not that Gust entertained any scruples on the subject, other than those which induced in him a rare regard for his own personal safety. There is always a certain element of risk to the assassin, for victims of deadly assault are seldom prone to go so far as to dispute the issue with the murderer. It was this chance of dispute which Gust preferred to forgo.

But now that the work was done the Swede aspired to the position of highest command among the mutineers. He had even gone so far as to appropriate and wear certain articles belonging to the murdered captain of the *Cowrie* —articles of apparel which bore upon them the badges and insignia of authority.

Kai Shang was peeved. He had no love for authority, and certainly not the slightest intention of submitting to the domination of an ordinary Swede sailor.

The seeds of discontent were, therefore, already planted in the camp of the mutineers of the *Cowrie* at the north edge of Jungle Island. But Kai Shang realized that he must act with circumspection, for Gust alone of the motley horde possessed sufficient knowledge of navigation to get them out of the South Atlantic and around the cape into more congenial waters where they might find a market for their ill-gotten wealth, and no questions asked.

The day before they sighted Jungle Island and discovered the little land-locked harbour upon the bosom of which the *Cowrie* now rode quietly at anchor, the watch had discovered the smoke and funnels of a warship upon the southern horizon.

The chance of being spoken and investigated by a man-of-war appealed not at all to any of them, so they put into hiding for a few days until the danger should have passed.

And now Gust did not wish to venture out to sea again. There was no telling, he insisted, but that the ship they had seen was actually searching for them. Kai Shang pointed out that such could not be the case since it was impossible for any human being other than themselves to have knowledge of what had transpired aboard the *Cowrie*.

But Gust was not to be persuaded. In his wicked heart he nursed a scheme whereby he might increase his share of the booty by something like one hundred per cent. He alone could sail the *Cowrie,* therefore the others could not leave Jungle Island without him; but what was there to prevent Gust, with just sufficient men to man the schooner, slipping away from Kai Shang, Momulla the Maori, and some half of the crew when opportunity presented?

It was for this opportunity that Gust waited. Some day there would come a moment when Kai Shang, Momulla, and three or four of the others would be absent from camp, exploring or hunting. The Swede racked his brain for some plan whereby he might successfully lure from the sight of the anchored ship those whom he had determined to abandon.

To this end he organized hunting party after hunting party, but always the devil of perversity seemed to enter the soul of Kai Shang, so that that wily celestial would never hunt except in the company of Gust himself.

One day Kai Shang spoke secretly with Momulla the Maori, pouring into the brown ear of his companion the suspicions which he harboured concerning the Swede. Momulla was for going immediately and running a long knife through the heart of the traitor.

It is true that Kai Shang had no other evidence than the natural cunning of his own knavish soul—but he imagined in the intentions of Gust what he himself would have been glad to accomplish had the means lain at hand.

But he dared not let Momulla slay the Swede, upon whom they depended to guide them to their destination. They decided, however, that it would do no harm to attempt to frighten Gust into acceding to their demands, and with this purpose in mind the Maori sought out the self-constituted commander of the party.

When he broached the subject of immediate departure Gust again raised his former objection—that the warship might very probably be patrolling the sea directly in their southern path, waiting for them to make the attempt to reach other waters.

Momulla scoffed at the fears of his fellow, pointing out that as no one aboard any warship knew of their mutiny there could be no reason why they should be suspected.

"Ah!" exclaimed Gust, "there is where you are wrong. There is where you are lucky that you have an educated man like me to tell you what to do. You are an ignorant savage, Momulla, and so you know nothing of wireless."

The Maori leaped to his feet and laid his hand upon the hilt of his knife.

"I am no savage," he shouted.

"I was only joking," the Swede hastened to explain. "We are old friends, Momulla; we cannot afford to quarrel, at least not while old Kai Shang is plotting to steal all the pearls from us. If he could find a man to navigate the *Cowrie* he would leave us in a minute. All his talk about getting away from here is just because he has some scheme in his head to get rid of us."

"But the wireless," asked Momulla. "What has the wireless to do with our remaining here?"

"Oh yes," replied Gust, scratching his head. He was wondering if the Maori were really so ignorant as to believe the preposterous lie he was about to unload upon him. "Oh yes! You see every warship is equipped with what they call a wireless apparatus. It lets them talk to other ships hundreds of miles away, and it lets them listen to all that is said on these other ships. Now, you see, when you fellows were shooting up the *Cowrie* you did a whole lot of loud talking, and there isn't any doubt but that that warship was a-lyin' off south of us listenin' to it all. Of course they might not have learned the name of the ship, but they heard enough to know that the crew of some ship was mutinying and killin' her officers. So you see they'll be waiting to search every ship they sight for a long time to come, and they may not be far away now,"

When he had ceased speaking the Swede strove to assume an air of composure that his listener might not have his suspicions aroused as to the truth of the statements that had just been made.

Momulla sat for some time in silence, eyeing Gust. At last he rose.

"You are a great liar," he said. "If you don't get us on our way by tomorrow you'll never have another chance to lie, for I heard two of the men saying that they'd like to run a knife into you and that if you kept them in this hole any longer they'd do it."

"Go and ask Kai Shang if there is not a wireless," replied Gust. "He will tell you that there is such a thing and that vessels can talk to one another across hundreds of miles of water. Then say to the two men who wish to kill me that if they do so they will never live to spend their share of the swag, for only I can get you safely to any port."

So Momulla went to Kai Shang and asked him if there was such an apparatus as a wireless by means of which ships could talk with each other at great distances, and Kai Shang told him that there was.

Momulla was puzzled; but still he wished to leave the island, and was willing to take his chances on the open sea rather than to remain longer in the monotony of the camp.

"If we only had someone else who could navigate a ship!" wailed Kai Shang.

That afternoon Momulla went hunting with two other Maoris. They hunted toward the south, and had not gone far from camp when they were surprised by the sound of voices ahead of them in the jungle.

They knew that none of their own men had preceded them, and as all were convinced that the island was un-inhabited, they were inclined to flee in terror on the hypothesis that the place was haunted—possibly by the ghosts of the murdered officers and men of the *Cowrie*.

But Momulla was even more curious than he was superstitious, and so he quelled his natural desire to flee from the supernatural. Motioning his companions to follow his example, he dropped to his hands and knees, crawling forward stealthily and with quakings of heart through the jungle in the direction from which came the voices of the unseen speakers.

Presently, at the edge of a little clearing, he halted, and there he breathed a deep sigh of relief, for plainly before him he saw two flesh-and-blood men sitting upon a fallen log and talking earnestly together.

One was Schneider, mate of the *Kincaid*, and the other was a seaman named Schmidt.

"I think we can do it, Schmidt," Schneider was saying. "A good canoe wouldn't be hard to build, and three of us could paddle it to the mainland in a day if the wind was right and the sea reasonably calm. There ain't no use waiting for the men to build a big enough boat to take the whole party, for they're sore now and sick of working like slaves all day long. It ain't none of our business anyway to save the Englishman. Let him look out for himself, says I." He paused for a moment, and then eyeing the other to note the effect of his next words, he continued, "But we might take the woman. It would be a shame to leave a nice-lookin' piece like she is in such a Gott-forsaken hole as this here island."

Schmidt looked up and grinned.

"So that's how she's blowin', is it?" he asked. "Why didn't you say so in the first place? Wot's in it for me if I help you?"

"She ought to pay us well to get her back to civilization," explained Schneider, "an' I tell you what I'll do, I'll just whack up with the two men that helps me. I'll take half an' they can divide the other half—you an' whoever the other bloke is. I'm sick of this place, an' the sooner I get out of it the better I'll like it. What do you say?"

"Suits me," replied Schmidt. "I wouldn't know how to reach the mainland myself, an' know that none o' the other fellows would, so's you're the only one what knows anything of navigation you're the fellow I'll tie to."

Momulla the Maori pricked up his ears. He had a smattering of every tongue that is spoken upon the seas, and more than a few times had he sailed on English ships, so that he understood fairly well all that had passed between Schneider and Schmidt since he had stumbled upon them.

He rose to his feet and stepped into the clearing. Schneider and his companion started as nervously as though a ghost had risen before them. Schneider reached for his revolver. Momulla raised his right hand, palm forward, as a sign of his pacific intentions.

"I am a friend," he said. "I heard you; but do not fear that I will reveal what you have said. I can help you, and you can help me." He was addressing Schneider. "You can navigate a ship, but you have no ship. We have a ship, but no one to navigate it. If you will come with us and ask no questions we will let you take the ship where you will after you have landed us at a certain port, the name of which we will give you later. You can take the woman of whom you speak, and we will ask no questions either. Is it a bargain?"

Schneider desired more information, and got as much as Momulla thought best to give him. Then the Maori suggested that they speak with Kai Shang. The two members of the *Kincaid*'s company followed Momulla and his fellows to a point in the jungle close by the camp of the mutineers. Here Momulla hid them while he went in search of Kai Shang, first admonishing his Maori companions to stand guard over the two sailors lest they change their minds and attempt to escape. Schneider and Schmidt were virtually prisoners, though they did not know it.

Presently Momulla returned with Kai Shang, to whom he had briefly narrated the details of the stroke of good fortune that had come to them. The Chinaman spoke at length with Schneider, until, notwithstanding his natural suspicion of the sincerity of all men, he became quite convinced that Schneider was quite as much of a rogue as himself and that the fellow was anxious to leave the island.

These two premises accepted there could be little doubt that Schneider would prove trustworthy in so far as accepting the command of the *Cowrie* was concerned; after that Kai Shang knew that he could find means to coerce the man into submission to his further wishes.

When Schneider and Schmidt left them and set out in the direction of their own camp, it was with feelings of far greater relief than they had experienced in many a day. Now at last they saw a feasible plan for leaving the island upon a seaworthy craft. There would be no more hard labour at shipbuilding, and no risking their lives upon a crudely built makeshift that would be quite as likely to go to the bottom as it would to reach the mainland.

Also, they were to have assistance in capturing the woman, or rather women, for when Momulla had learned that there was a black woman in the other camp he had insisted that she be brought along as well as the white woman.

As Kai Shang and Momulla entered their camp, it was with a realization that they no longer needed Gust. They marched straight to the tent in which they might expect to find him at that hour of the day, for though it would have been more comfortable for the entire party to remain aboard the ship, they had mutually decided that it would be safer for all concerned were they to pitch their camp ashore.

Each knew that in the heart of the others was sufficient treachery to make it unsafe for any member of the party to go ashore leaving the others in possession of the *Cowrie*, so not more than two or three men at a time were ever permitted aboard the vessel unless all the balance of the company was there too.

As the two crossed toward Gust's tent the Maori felt the edge of his long knife with one grimy, calloused thumb. The Swede would have felt far from comfortable could he have seen this significant action, or read what was passing amid the convolutions of the brown man's cruel brain.

Now it happened that Gust was at that moment in the tent occupied by the cook, and this tent stood but a few feet from his own. So that he heard the approach of Kai Shang and Momulla, though he did not, of course, dream that it had any special significance for him.

Chance had it, though, that he glanced out of the doorway of the cook's tent at the very moment that Kai Shang and Momulla approached the entrance to his, and he thought that he noted a stealthiness in their movements that comported poorly with amicable or friendly intentions, and then, just as they two slunk within the interior, Gust caught a glimpse of the long knife which Momulla the Maori was then carrying behind his back.

The Swede's eyes opened wide, and a funny little sensation assailed the roots of his hairs. Also he turned almost white beneath his tan. Quite precipitately he left the cook's tent. He was not one who required a detailed exposition of intentions that were quite all too obvious.

As surely as though he had heard them plotting, he knew that Kai Shang and Momulla had come to take his life. The knowledge that he alone could navigate the *Cowrie* had, up to now, been sufficient assurance of his safety; but quite evidently something had occurred of which he had no knowledge that would make it quite worth the while of his co-conspirators to eliminate him.

Without a pause Gust darted across the beach and into the jungle. He was afraid of the jungle; uncanny noises that were indeed frightful came forth from its recesses—the tangled mazes of the mysterious country back of the beach.

But if Gust was afraid of the jungle he was far more afraid of Kai Shang and Momulla. The dangers of the jungle were more or less problematical, while the danger that menaced him at the hands of his companions was a perfectly well-known quantity, which might be expressed in terms of a few inches of cold steel, or the coil of a light rope. He had seen Kai Shang garrotte a man at Pai-sha in a dark alleyway back of Loo Kotai's place. He feared the rope, therefore, more than he did the knife of the Maori; but he feared them both too much to remain within reach of either. Therefore he chose the pitiless jungle.

21

The Law of the Jungle

I N Tarzan's camp, by dint of threats and promised rewards, the ape-man had finally succeeded in getting the hull of a large skiff almost completed. Much of the work he and Mugambi had done with their own hands in addition to furnishing the camp with meat.

Schneider, the mate, had been doing considerable grumbling, and had at last openly deserted the work and gone off into the jungle with Schmidt to hunt. He said that he wanted a rest, and Tarzan, rather than add to the unplesantness which already made camp life almost unendurable, had permitted the two men to depart without a remonstrance.

Upon the following day, however, Schneider affected a feeling of remorse for his action, and set to work with a will upon the skiff. Schmidt also worked good-naturedly, and Lord Greystoke congratulated himself that at last the men had awakened to the necessity for the labour which was being asked of them and to their obligations to the balance of the party.

It was with a feeling of greater relief than he had experienced for many a day that he set out that noon to hunt deep in the jungle for a herd of small deer which Schneider reported that he and Schmidt had seen there the day before.

The direction in which Schneider had reported seeing the deer was toward the south-west, and to that point the ape-man swung easily through the tangled verdure of the forest.

And as he went there approached from the north a half-dozen ill-featured men who went stealthily through the jungle as go men bent upon the commission of a wicked act.

They thought that they travelled unseen; but behind them, almost from the moment they quitted their own camp, a tall man crept upon their trail. In the man's eyes were hate and fear, and a great curiosity. Why went Kai Shang and Momulla and the others thus stealthily toward the south? What did they expect to find there? Gust shook his low-browed head in perplexity. But he would know. He would follow them and learn their plans, and then if he could thwart them he would—that went without question.

At first he had thought that they searched for him; but finally his better judgment assured him that such could not be the case, since they had accomplished all they really desired by chasing him out of camp. Never would Kai Shang or Momulla go to such pains to slay him or another unless it would put money into their pockets, and as Gust had no money it was evident that they were searching for someone else.

Presently the party he trailed came to a halt. Its members concealed themselves in the foilage bordering the game trail along which they had come. Gust, that he might the better observe, clambered into the branches of a tree to the rear of them, being careful that the leafy fronds hid him from the view of his erstwhile mates.

He had not long to wait before he saw a strange white man approach carefully along the trail from the south.

At sight of the newcomer Momulla and Kai Shang arose from their places of concealment and greeted him. Gust could not overhear what passed between them. Then the man returned in the direction from which he had come.

He was Schneider. Nearing his camp he circled to the opposite side of it, and presently came running in breathlessly. Excitedly he hastened to Mugambi.

"Quick!" he cried. "Those apes of yours have caught Schmidt and will kill him if we do not hasten to his aid. You alone can call them off. Take Jones and Sullivan—you may need help—and get to him as quick as you can. Follow the game trail south for about a mile. I will remain here. I am too spent with running to go back with you," and the mate of the *Kincaid* threw himself upon the ground, panting as though he was almost done for.

Mugambi hesitated. He had been left to guard the two women. He did not know what to do, and then Jane Clayton, who had heard Schneider's story, added her pleas to those of the mate.

"Do not delay," she urged. "We shall be all right here.

Mr. Schneider will remain with us. Go, Mugambi. The poor fellow must be saved."

Schmidt, who lay hidden in a bush at the edge of the camp, grinned. Mugambi, heeding the commands of his mistress, though still doubtful of the wisdom of his action, started off toward the south, with Jones and Sullivan at his heels.

No sooner had he disappeared than Schmidt rose and darted north into the jungle, and a few minutes later the face of Kai Shang of Fachan appeared at the edge of the clearing. Schneider saw the Chinaman, and motioned to him that the coast was clear.

Jane Clayton and the Mosula woman were sitting at the opening of the former's tent, their backs toward the approaching ruffians. The first intimation that either had of the presence of strangers in camp was the sudden appearance of a half-dozen ragged villains about them.

"Come!" said Kai Shang, motioning that the two arise and follow him.

Jane Clayton sprang to her feet and looked about for Schneider, only to see him standing behind the newcomers, a grin upon his face. At his side stood Schmidt. Instantly she saw that she had been made the victim of a plot.

"What is the meaning of this?" she asked, addressing the mate.

"It means that we have found a ship and that we can now escape from Jungle Island," replied the man.

"Why did you send Mugambi and the others into the jungle?" she inquired.

"They are not coming with us—only you and I, and the Mosula woman."

"Come!" repeated Kai Shang, and seized Jane Clayton's wrist.

One of the Maoris grasped the black woman by the arm, and when she would have screamed struck her across the mouth.

Mugambi raced through the jungle toward the south. Jones and Sullivan trailed far behind. For a mile he continued upon his way to the relief of Schmidt, but no signs saw he of the missing man or of any of the apes of Akut.

At last he halted and called aloud the summons which he and Tarzan had used to hail the great anthropoids. There was no response. Jones and Sullivan came up with the black warrior as the latter stood voicing his weird call. For another half-mile the black searched, calling occasionally. Finally the truth flashed upon him, and then, like a frightened deer, he wheeled and dashed back toward camp. Arriving there, it was but a moment before full confirmation of his fears was impressed upon him. Lady Greystoke and the Mosula woman were gone. So, likewise, was Schneider.

When Jones and Sullivan joined Mugambi he would have killed them in his anger, thinking them parties to the plot; but they finally succeeded in partially convincing him that they had known nothing of it.

As they stood speculating upon the probable whereabouts of the women and their abductor, and the purpose which Schneider had in mind in taking them from camp, Tarzan of the Apes swung from the branches of a tree and crossed the clearing toward them.

His keen eyes detected at once that something was radically wrong, and when he had heard Mugambi's story his jaws clicked angrily together as he knitted his brows in thought.

What could the mate hope to accomplish by taking Jane Clayton from a camp upon a small island from which there was no escape from the vengeance of Tarzan? The ape-man could not believe the fellow such a fool, and then a slight realization of the truth dawned upon him.

Schneider would not have committed such an act unless he had been reasonably sure that there was a way by which he could quit Jungle Island with his prisoners. But why had he taken the black woman as well? There must have been others, one of whom wanted the dusky female.

"Come," said Tarzan, "there is but one thing to do now, and that is to follow their trail."

As he finished speaking a tall, ungainly figure emerged from the jungle north of the camp. He came straight toward the four men. He was an entire stranger to all of them, not one of whom had dreamed that another human being than those of their own camp dwelt upon the unfriendly shores of Jungle Island.

It was Gust. He came directly to the point.

"Your women were stolen," he said. "If you want ever to see them again, come quickly and follow me. If we do not hurry the *Cowrie* will be standing out to sea by the time we reach her anchorage."

"Who are you?" asked Tarzan. "What do you know of the theft of my wife and the black woman?"

"I heard Kai Shang and Momulla the Maori plot with two men of your camp. They had chased me from our camp, and would have killed me. Now I will get even with them. Come!"

Gust led the four men of the *Kincaid*'s camp at a rapid

trot through the jungle toward the north. Would they come to the sea in time? But a few more minutes would answer the question.

And when at last the little party did break through the last of the screening foliage, and the harbour and the ocean lay before them, they realized that fate had been most cruelly unkind, for the *Dowrie* was already under sail and moving slowly out of the mouth of the habour into the open sea.

What were they to do? Tarzan's broad chest rose and fell to the force of his pent emotions. The last blow seemed to have fallen, and if ever in all his life Tarzan of the Apes had had occason to abandon hope it was now that he saw the ship bearing his wife to some frightful fate moving gracefully over the rippling water, so very near and yet so hideously far away.

In silence he stood watching the vessel. He saw it turn toward the east and finally disappear around a headland on its way he knew not whither. Then he dropped upon his haunches and buried his face in his hands.

It was after dark that the five men returned to the camp on the east shore. The night was hot and sultry. No slightest breeze ruffled the foliage of the trees or rippled the mirror-like surface of the ocean. Only a gentle swell rolled softly in upon the beach.

Never had Tarzan seen the great Atlantic so ominously at peace. He was standing at the edge of the beach gazing out to sea in the direction of the mainland, his mind filled with sorrow and hopelessness, when from the jungle close behind the camp came the uncanny wail of a panther.

There was a familiar note in the weird cry, and almost mechanically Tarzan turned his head and answered. A moment later the tawny figure of Sheeta slunk out into the half-light of the beach. There was no moon, but the sky was brilliant with stars. Silently the savage brute came to the side of the man. It had been long since Tarzan had seen his old fighting companion, but the soft purr was sufficient to assure him that the animal still recalled the bonds which had united them in the past.

The ape-man let his fingers fall upon the beast's coat, and as Sheeta pressed close against his leg he caressed and fondled the wicked head while his eyes continued to search the blackness of the waters.

Presently he started. What was that? He strained his eyes into the night. Then he turned and called aloud to the men smoking upon their blankets in the camp. They came running to his side; but Gust hesitated when he saw the nature of Tarzan's companion.

"Look!" cried Tarzan. "A light! A ship's light! It must be the *Cowrie*. They are becalmed." And then with an exclamation of renewed hope, "We can reach them! The skiff will carry us easily."

Gust demurred. "They are well armed," he warned. "We could not take the ship—just five of us."

"There are six now," replied Tarzan, pointing to Sheeta, "and we can have more still in a half-hour. Sheeta is the equivalent of twenty men, and the few others I can bring will add full a hundred to our fighting strength. You do not know them."

The ape-man turned and raised his head toward the jungle, while there pealed from his lips, time after time, the fearsome cry of the bull-ape who would summon his fellows.

Presently from the jungle came an answering cry, and then another and another. Gust shuddered. Among what sort of creatures had fate thrown him? Were not Kai Shang and Momulla to be preferred to this great white giant who stroked a panther and called to the beasts of the jungle?

In a few minutes the apes of Akut came crashing through the underbrush and out upon the beach, while in the meantime the five men had been struggling with the unwieldy bulk of the skiff's hull.

By dint of Herculean efforts they had managed to get it to the water's edge. The oars from the two small boats of the *Kincaid*, which had been washed away by an off-shore wind the very night that the party had landed, had been in use to support the canvas of the sailcloth tents. These were hastily requisitioned, and by the time Akut and his followers came down to the water all was ready for embarkation.

Once again the hideous crew entered the service of their master, and without question took up their places in the skiff. The four men, for Gust could not be prevailed upon to accompany the party, fell to the oars, using them paddlewise, while some of the apes followed their example, and presently the ungainly skiff was moving quietly out to sea in the direction of the light which rose and fell gently with the swell.

A sleepy sailor kept a poor vigil upon the *Cowrie*'s deck, while in the cabin below Schneider paced up and down arguing with Jane Clayton. The woman had found a revolver in a table drawer in the room in which she had been locked, and now she kept the mate of the *Kincaid* at bay with the weapon.

The Mosula woman kneeled behind her, while Schneider

paced up and down before the door, threatening and pleading and promising, but all to no avail. Presently from the
deck above came a shout of warning and a shot. For an instant
Jane Clayton relaxed her vigilance, and turned her eyes
toward the cabin skylight. Simultaneously Schneider was
upon her.

The first intimation the watch had that there was another
craft within a thousand miles of the *Crowie* came when he
saw the head and shoulders of a man poked over the ship's
side. Instantly the fellow sprang to his feet with a cry and
levelled his revolver at the intruder. It was his cry and the
subsequent report of the revolver which threw Jane Clayton
off her guard.

Upon deck the quiet of fancied security soon gave place
to the wildest pandemonium. The crew of the *Crowie*
rushed above armed with revolvers, cutlasses, and the long
knives that many of them habitually wore; but the alarm
had come too late. Already the beasts of Tarzan were upon
the ship's deck, with Tarzan and the two men of the *Kincaid's*
crew.

In the face of the frightful beasts the courage of the
mutineers wavered and broke. Those with revolvers fired a
few scattering shots and then raced for some place of sup-
posed safety. Into the shrouds went some; but the apes of
Akut were more at home there than they.

Screaming with terror the Maoris were dragged from their
lofty perches. The beasts, uncontrolled by Tarzan who had
gone in search of Jane, loosed the full fury of their savage
natures upon the unhappy wretches who fell into their
clutches.

Sheeta, in the meanwhile, had felt his great fangs sink into
but a single jugular. For a moment he mauled the corpse,
and then he spied Kai Shang darting down the companion-
way toward his cabin.

With a shrill scream Sheeta was after him—a scream
which awoke an almost equally uncanny cry in the throat of
the terrorstricken Chinaman.

But Kai Shang reached his cabin a fraction of a second
ahead of the panther, and leaping within slammed the door
—just too late. Sheeta's great body hurtled against it before
the catch engaged, and a moment later Kai Shang was gib-
bering and shrieking in the back of an upper berth.

Lightly Sheeta sprang after his victim, and presently the
wicked days of Kai Shang of Fachan were ended, and
Sheeta was gorging himself upon tough and stringy flesh.

A moment scarcely had elapsed after Schneider leaped
upon Jane Clayton and wrenched the revolver from her hand,

when the door of the cabin opened and a tall and half-naked white man stood framed within the portal.

Silently he leaped across the cabin. Schneider felt sinewy fingers at his throat. He turned his head to see who had attacked him, and his eyes went wide when he saw the face of the ape-man close above his own.

Grimly the fingers tightened upon the mate's throat. He tried to scream, to plead, but no sound came forth. His eyes protruded as he struggled for freedom, for breath, for life.

Jane Clayton seized her husband's hands and tried to drag them from the throat of the dying man; but Tarzan only shook his head.

"Not again," he said quietly. "Before have I permitted scoundrels to live, only to suffer and to have you suffer for my mercy. This time we shall make sure of one scoundrel —sure that he will never again harm us or another," and with a sudden wrench he twisted the neck of the perfidious mate until there was a sharp crack, and the man's body lay limp and motionless in the ape-man's grasp. With a gesture of disgust Tarzan tossed the corpse aside. Then he returned to the deck, followed by Jane and the Mosula woman.

The battle there was over. Schmidt and Momulla and two others alone remained alive of all the company of the *Cowrie*, for they had found sanctuary in the forecastle. The others had died, horribly, and as they deserved, beneath the fangs and talons of the beasts of Tarzan, and in the morning the sun rose on a grisly sight upon the deck of the unhappy *Cowrie*; but this time the blood which stained her white planking was the blood of the guilty and not of the innocent.

Tarzan brought forth the men who had hidden in the forecastle, and without promises of immunity from punishment forced them to help work the vessel—the only alternative was immediate death.

A stiff breeze had risen with the sun, and with canvas spread the *Cowrie* set in toward Jungle Island, where a few hours later, Tarzan picked up Gust and bid farewell to Sheeta and the apes of Akut, for here he set the beasts ashore to pursue the wild and natural life they loved so well; nor did they lose a moment's time in disappearing into the cool depths of their beloved jungle.

That they knew that Tarzan was to leave them may be doubted—except possibly in the case of the more intelligent Akut, who alone of all the others remained upon the beach as the small boat drew away toward the schooner, carrying his savage lord and master from him.

And as long as their eyes could span the distance, Jane and Tarzan, standing upon the deck, saw the lonely figure of the shaggy anthropoid motionless upon the surf-beaten sands of Jungle Island.

It was three days later that the *Crowie* fell in with H.M. sloop-of-war *Shorewater*, through whose wireless Lord Greystoke soon got in communication with London. Thus he learned that which filled his and his wife's heart with joy and thanksgiving—little Jack was safe at Lord Greystoke's town house.

It was not until they reached London that they learned the details of the remarkable chain of circumstances that had preserved the infant unharmed.

It developed that Rokoff, fearing to take the child aboard the *Kincaid* by day, had hidden it in a low den where nameless infants were harboured, intending to carry it to the steamer after dark.

His confederate and chief lieutenant, Paulvitch, true to the long years of teaching of his wily master, had at last succumbed to the treachery and greed that had always marked his superior, and, lured by the thoughts of the immense ransom that he might win by returning the child unharmed, had divulged the secret of its parentage to the woman who maintained the foundling asylum. Through her he had arranged for the substitution of another infant, knowing full well that never until it was too late would Rokoff suspect the trick that had been played upon him.

The woman had promised to keep the child until Paulvitch returned to England; but she, in turn, had been tempted to betray her trust by the lure of gold, and so had opened negotiations with Lord Greystoke's solicitors for the return of the child.

Esmeralda, the old Negro nurse whose absence on a vacation in America at the time of the abduction of little Jack had been attributed by her as the cause of the calamity, had returned and positively identified the infant.

The ransom had been paid, and within ten days of the date of his kidnapping the future Lord Greystoke, none the worse for his experience, had been returned to his father's home.

And so that last and greatest of Nikolas Rokoff's many rascalities had not only miserably miscarried through the treachery he had taught his only friend, but it had resulted in the arch-villain's death, and given to Lord and Lady Greystoke a peace of mind that neither could ever have felt so long as the vital spark remained in the body of the Russian and his malign mind was free to formulate new atrocities against them.

Rokoff was dead, and while the fate of Paulvitch was unknown, they had every reason to believe that he had succumbed to the dangers of the jungle where last they had seen him—the malicious tool of his master.

And thus, in so far as they might know, they were to be freed for ever from the menace of these two men—the only enemies which Tarzan of the Apes ever had had occasion to fear, because they struck at him cowardly blows, through those he loved.

It was a happy family party that were reunited in Greystoke House the day that Lord Greystoke and his lady landed upon English soil from the deck of the *Shorewater*.

Accompanying them were Mugambi and the Mosula woman whom he had found in the bottom of the canoe that night upon the bank of the little tributary of the Ugambi.

The woman had preferred to cling to her new lord and master rather than return to the marriage she had tried to escape.

Tarzan had proposed to them that they might find a home upon his vast African estates in the land of the Waziri, where they were to be sent as soon as opportunity presented itself.

Possibly we shall see them all there amid the savage romance of the grim jungle and the great plains where Tarzan of the Apes loves best to be.

Who knows?
